Beyond the Plain and Simple

Beyond the Plain and Simple

A Patchwork of Amish Lives

Pauline Stevick

Illustrations by Freiman Stoltzfus

The Kent State University Press
Kent, Ohio

© 2006 by The Kent State University Press, Kent, Ohio 44242

ALL RIGHTS RESERVED

Library of Congress Catalog Card Number 2006016312

ISBN-10: 0-87338-880-1

ISBN-13: 978-0-87338-880-1

Manufactured in the United States of America

10 09 08 07 06   5 4 3 2 1

LIBRARY OF CONGRESS CATALOGING-IN-PUBLICATION DATA

Stevick, Pauline, 1938–

Beyond the plain and simple : a patchwork of Amish lives / Pauline Stevick ;
illustrations by Freiman Stoltzfus.

p. cm.

Includes bibliographical references and index.

ISBN-13: 978-0-87338-880-1 (hardcover : alk. paper) ∞

ISBN-10: 0-87338-880-1 (hardcover : alk. paper) ∞

1. Amish—United States—Social life and customs—Anecdotes.   2. Amish—United
States—Biography—Anecdotes.   3. Community life—United States—Anecdotes.
4. Country life—United States—Anecdotes.   5. United States—Social life and customs—Anecdotes.   6. United States—Biography—Anecdotes.   7. Stevick, Pauline,
1938– —Travel—United States.   8. United States—Description and travel.   I. Title.

E184.M45S74 2006

289.7'3—dc22   20006016312

British Library Cataloging-in-Publication data are available.

Foreword

by Donald B. Kraybill

As one of the more colorful subcultures in American life, the Amish intrigue us. As outsiders we are drawn to them because of their strong bonds of community, their commitment to family, their strong sense of place, and their stubborn resistance to the mania of technology that often drives modern life. Although we are drawn to them, we rarely have the opportunity to hear genuine Amish voices or listen to the joys and struggles of daily life in Amish homes across the country. In *Beyond the Plain and Simple*, Pauline Stevick introduces us to many Amish people in different states and communities. She takes us backstage in Amish society and narrates a series of vignettes that provide profound insight into the beauty and the pathos of this distinctive religious community.

With an engaging and inviting writing style, Stevick describes many of the features of Amish life with warmth, sensitivity, and respect. Her writing is not fettered with abstract academic concepts, nor does she sensationalize or stereotype Amish life. In an even-handed style, she introduces us to many common Amish practices as well as to the diversity of Amish life. Instead of focusing on just one family or one community, we hear stories from many different communities and church traditions. The potpourri of stories provides a frank and candid window to the real-life struggles of real people, not the stereotypical postcard figures who are sporting beards and bonnets.

At first blush, the Amish seem so far away from us, living in a different cultural world far from the cosmopolitan culture of urban life. Nevertheless, Stevick takes us on an Amish journey that reveals the ways that we share many of their struggles and concerns. Perhaps most important is the sense of Amish agency that emerges from the text. We hear real Amish people talking about their delights and fears. And as we hear them speak we realize that although we stand on the other side of a cultural fence, all of us—Amish and English—share common bonds of humanity. That, perhaps, is the most important contribution of this intriguing collection of stories that take us far beyond the plain and simple postcard stereotypes.

For Rich, Mark, Don, and Dorothy—
who believed in me

Contents

A Historical Amish Primer

The Amish, part of the "plain people"—so called because of their plain dress and simple lifestyle—never forget their origins in the Reformation in Europe.

The *Amish* (pronounced Ah-mish), the *Mennonites*, and the *Brethren* are descendants of the *Anabaptist* wing of the Reformation, which had its roots in sixteenth-century Switzerland. Onlookers derisively employed the term Anabaptist to describe a group of followers of the reformer Ulrich Zwingli who believed he and others had not gone far enough in their reforming practices. After deciding that his practice of infant baptism was contrary to scripture, they rebaptized each other despite their having been baptized as infants. These early Anabaptists insisted that neither church nor parents had the right to baptize an individual unless the individual himself or herself confessed faith in Christ, hence the term *believers baptism*. For this and other beliefs, based on their determination to interpret and live out scripture as literally as possible, many Anabaptists were severely persecuted, imprisoned, tortured, and killed during the more than two hundred years that followed.

About a century following the original rebaptizing incident, a group of Swiss Anabaptists (Swiss Brethren) who migrated to the Alsatian area of what is now France decided that some of the practices of the Anabaptists they had left behind in Switzerland needed to be reformed. Under the influence of Jacob Amman, they began conducting communion semiannually rather than annually, included the custom of feet washing along with communion, and insisted on a more severe social shunning of disobedient members rather than mere expulsion from religious services. This group subsequently decided on a plainer mode of dress as well. Garnering the support of these followers and others in Bern and the Palatinate region of Germany, Jacob Amman excommunicated the less conservative Swiss Brethren who disagreed with him. Despite attempts at reconciliation, the split was not repaired. Jacob Amman's group became known as Amish, whereas the group they left behind was later called Mennonists or Mennonites, after an influential Dutch leader, Menno Simons.

The Lancaster County, Pennsylvania, Amish group is the most well-known of the Amish enclaves, but it is not the largest.

Like many other persecuted religious persons, Mennonites and Amish immigrated to Pennsylvania during the eighteenth century. Both groups settled in Lancaster County, where they flourished, and later many migrated to many other states as well. While the one hundred-plus districts in Lancaster represent the oldest grouping of Amish, the largest is located in Holmes, Wayne, and Stark counties in Ohio and the third largest is in Elkhart and LaGrange counties in Indiana. However, Amish groups are clustered in areas known to them as settlements in twenty-seven states and Ontario. Within these settlements they are organized in districts, which typically consist of twenty-five to thirty-five families, although in the smaller settlements the number of families may be far fewer. Theoretically, a bishop, two ministers, and a deacon oversee each district, although this does not always work out in practice.

While all Amish groups share a core belief system and similar code of conduct, they are not identical and sometimes do not "affiliate" with one another.

All Amish groups embrace the basic tenets of the Amish faith, which in addition to adult baptism and a literal obedience to Christ and his teaching, include the separation from the world, a nonviolent lifestyle, and membership in a "covenant community." In general, the Amish embrace simplicity and tradition, are suspicious of the effects of new technology on their covenant community, and change beliefs and practices very slowly. Rather than having a written "discipline" as some church groups do, the Amish agree together upon their mutual system of conduct, or specific "rules," which collectively is known as the Ordnung and which is transmitted orally. The Ordnungs of districts and settlements that affiliate with each other—that is, who exchange preachers and "fellowship" with one another—will be almost identical, whereas a careful observer will note differences in dress style (still plain) and level of technology permitted among nonaffiliating settlements. Of course, the similarities are much more marked than the differences.

The largest group of Amish, the Old Order Amish, are the "guardians" of the traditions of the past. More progressive groups include, among others, the New Order Amish, who still meet in houses for their services, still use horses and carriages but in some settlements allow electricity; and the Beachy Amish Church, whose members drive cars and use electricity and who have meetinghouses and often espouse a more "evangelical" concept of spirituality. Several other significant aspects of doctrine and practice distinguish these two groups from their more conservative cousins. Distinguishing between the various groups is confusing for outsiders, who may also encounter plainly dressed Old Order Mennonites driving horses and carriages but who are not affiliated with the Amish.[1]

Contemporary Anabaptists can be classified into four major groupings: Amish, Brethren, Hutterites, and Mennonites. Although members of some of these groups are "plain," not all are. Likewise, not all eschew modern technology. Members of some of the major Mennonite and Brethren groups wear clothing similar to that of many mainstream Americans and use modern machinery and technology but embrace most or all of the Anabaptist theological tenets. The author of this work is a member of the Brethren in Christ denomination, an offshoot of the Mennonites but classified under the Brethren group because of its strong pietistic emphasis.[2]

---

1. Donald B. Kraybill, *The Riddle of Amish Culture*, rev. ed. (Baltimore, Md.: Johns Hopkins Univ. Press, 2001), 3–8.

2. For a thorough treatment of present-day Anabaptism, see Donald B. Kraybill and C. Nelson Hostetter, *Anabaptist World USA* (Scottdale, Pa.: Herald Press), 2001. The classification of the four contemporary Anabaptist groups comes from this book.

Introduction

Will the Real Amish Please Come Forward?
(Or, How This Book Came to Be Written)

$\mathcal{S}$lowly the long line of gray, horse-drawn carriages wends up the hill past fields of young spears of corn and fragrant alfalfa, through the narrow gate to the cemetery with its plain grave markers. Clad almost exclusively in black, the occupants disembark and gather silently around the mound of dirt marking a recently dug grave. The men somberly bear a handmade wooden casket to the site, and the singsong tones of the minister commence across the still air.

At the far end of the cemetery, several figures in oversized T-shirts, shorts, and sneakers slip from behind a large maple, brandishing cameras. They hastily snap three or four pictures, then turn and dash across the adjoining field, their laughter stinging the ears of the bereaved whose privacy they have transgressed. Not only are these tourists showing a lack of respect for the Amish mourners, they are also violating the mourners' religious beliefs. Since the Amish interpret picture taking as a transgression of the commandment not to make graven images, taking a photograph without permission at a time of grief is particularly offensive.

How crass. How utterly insensitive and rude. I would ridicule the camera-toting intruders, but I bite my tongue, remembering my own curiosity regarding the Amish way of life. I vow to express it less offensively.

Consider another scene. The speaker is briefing his visiting Amish audience on the history of his own Amish settlement. He gives the names of its early emigrants: Zooks, Hochstetlers, Fishers, Beilers, Millers, and Masts, names familiar in many Amish communities. The first settler, he points out, crossed the state in a covered wagon. His own ancestors are buried in a local cemetery, which they will visit. One of the farms they will soon be passing on our bus tour, he remarks, has been in the same family for seven generations, and nearly all of the men presently living in the community are employed as farmers. He recites the occupations of those who do not farm: a few carpenters, harness makers, a broom maker, some weavers, some sawyers. He lists the names of the early bishops and ministers and discusses some of the reasons for several schisms that occurred in the last century. Since this settlement is one of the few that have meetinghouses for worship services, the tour includes a stop at one of them. We gather inside, sitting on hard, wooden benches as our leader continues his talk.

My husband and I are among a handful of non-Amish listeners to this history lesson. We watch as this group from an Amish settlement several counties away responds to his account with nods and polite questions.

Then suddenly the questions turn personal. "How did you find your wife?" one listener inquires. "Why did you have to go to another county to find a wife? Why couldn't you find one in your own settlement?"

Taken by surprise, our speaker pauses momentarily. Suddenly an Amish listener observes the irony in the situation. "We sound like a bunch of tourists," he exclaims.

"Yeah," calls an Amishman from across the room. "Take your picture?"

The entire assemblage breaks into laughter, demonstrating the ability and willingness to look at both themselves and the tourists who watch them from an outside perspective.

Who are they, these plain people who, despite curious and often intrusive stares from outsiders, pursue their quiet and simple way of life? How does their culture, which appears to be a century or more behind the times, manage not only to exist, but also to thrive? Has the Amish insistence on faith and community brought them the contentment that many members of twenty-first-century American society seem to lack? How accurate are the images of the Amish presented in the tourist brochures? What is it really like to be Amish?

Questions like these proliferate as the Amish continue to be objects of popular interest. The hundreds of thousands of tourists who visit the major Amish settlements in Holmes and Wayne counties in Ohio, Lancaster County in Pennsylvania, and Elkhart and LaGrange counties in Indiana attest to the popularity of Amish watching. An increasing number of television documentaries in recent years, most notably Lucy Walker's 2002 documentary *The Devil's Playground* and the UPN 2004 television series *Amish in the City,* have garnered considerable interest among viewers. And the Amish themselves express curiosity regarding the customs of other Amish settlements, as the foregoing incident demonstrates.

While much of the media attention to the Amish is positive (the 1985 movie *Witness* and many coffee-table books) and other is negative *(The Devil's Playground),* none of it compares to the treatment of their Anabaptist ancestors in Europe during the sixteenth and early seventeenth centuries. At that time hundreds of Anabaptists (Swiss Brethren, Mennonites, and Amish) were hunted down by state and church authorities, then tortured and burned at the stake for their "extreme" and "heretical" religious beliefs. After the split between the Amish and the Swiss Brethren occurred in 1693, the Amish continued to be deeply influenced by the memories of these persecutions, which were recorded in *Martyrs Mirror*, a book found in most Amish homes today.

But, of course, the social and religious climate in the areas of the United States where the Amish now live is vastly different from that of Europe during the Reformation. All kinds of belief systems coexist in a country where pluralism has become a byword and where tolerance is extolled as a supreme virtue. As long as they maintain their simple rural ways and no major war inflames the public against their stubborn pacifism, the Amish are treated as quaint but interesting anachronisms from the pages of history. They are often viewed as harmless relics from the past, not unlike the figures in "living history" enactments featured at Williamsburg or Plimouth Plantation.

Until very recently, most people formed their impressions about Amish life from magazine articles and travel brochures touting the Amish country of the large—and lucrative—tourist centers in Pennsylvania, Ohio, or Indiana, or from the dramatic photographs and paintings that comprise the oversized, expensive books purchased in these centers and later displayed prominently on coffee tables. Frequently, such portrayals are idealistic, lauding the bucolic innocence of a people who have rejected the complexities of the modern world and who have retained a wholesomeness that results from their religious devotion and from their simple, rural, collectivist way of life.

These images feature barefooted Amish youths with blunt, Dutch-boy haircuts driving cows to pasture in the pale mist of dawn; wide-eyed children peering inquisitively from the backs of horse-drawn carriages; parents and children diligently working together planting corn or harvesting hay; white-aproned, dark-stockinged maidens dressed in their Sunday best strolling down quiet country lanes, their hair drawn tightly back and tucked under white organdy "coverings"; somberly dressed, venerable patriarchs in broad-brimmed straw hats contemplating the worth of stock at a horse auction; patchwork patterns of immaculate fields, farmhouses, and barns; and—of course—wide-angled views portraying the beehive busyness of a legendary barn raising.

Such scenes may prompt some onlookers to contemplate abandoning their twentieth-century conveniences in favor of the storybook happiness displayed before them. Many are motivated to vacation in places where businesses capitalize on the Amish presence and hawk everything from Amish quilts and Amish shoofly pie to Amish buggy rides. "Amish" anything sells.

I, too, was captivated by an article on the Lancaster County, Pennsylvania, Amish in the August 1965 *National Geographic.* A few weeks later my husband and I bicycled through the Pennsylvania Dutch country surrounding New Holland, Intercourse, and Bird-in-Hand. We ate shoofly pie, pedaled past water wheels that drove well pumps, stopped at farm stands to purchase tomatoes and sweet corn, and surreptitiously snapped a few photographs of Amish buggies passing a *Grossdawdy Haus,* the section of a farmhouse added for the older generation of an Amish family. We were enchanted not only with the Amish but also with the serene fecundity of Lancaster County.

A year later we moved there, and for the next dozen years we resided in or near "Amish country." From our house we could hear the staccato clip-clop of the horses' hooves against the asphalt pavement. As we drove behind those slow-moving carriages on nearby roads, we began to understand why some of the local residents were irritated, although we were much too fascinated with the Amish to be annoyed. (Only after riding in them much later did I discover just how fragile those carriages are compared to the tons of steel that rush impatiently—and often rudely—past them.)

Slowly I began to realize that the images of the Amish that some of my neighbors held differed from those portrayed in the coffee-table books or on the movie screen. Although Amish and English—their term for non-Amish persons—live side by side, and although they speak with each other and sometimes work together, the English frequently do not understand their Amish neighbors very well. Because the Amish set out to be separate from the world, they limit their interaction with those whose ways they deem to be "worldly." They determine that such persons will have little influence on their offspring.

Soon I began to hear frequent complaints about the grooves on the road created by the horses' hooves, about the standoffishness of the Amish, and especially about their inconsistencies. "They won't spend their money for their own telephones and they say it's wrong to have one, but they don't seem at all bothered by using ours," was a common grievance. A similar complaint came from neighbors who were irritated by frequent requests for car rides to places where the Amish could not go quickly enough with their horsepower.

Mainstream Americans often fail to understand the reasoning behind the apparent inconsistencies in the choice of technology and machinery, such as telephones or generators. They do not recognize that the Amish refuse to be controlled by technology, but that they instead choose to control it. Many Amish people resonate with some of mainstream society's prophetic voices, which warn that unbridled technology can be destructive to one's peace, can alienate humans from the earth, and can destroy family cohesion. And since the Amish cherish their separatist way of life and feel little need to reveal or defend it to outsiders, the majority of tourists and locals never really comprehend this aspect of "Amishness." But mainstream American parents who have wrestled with controlling a teenager's time on the telephone, use of the family car, or the content and duration of television viewing and Internet interaction may envy Amish parents who do not share these pressures.

Another accusation some of their English neighbors make against the Amish is that they are dirty. In a local dentist's office the employees declare that they can tell when an Amish person enters the reception room by the smell. The telltale odor of kerosene tends to linger on clothing, and when it combines with smells from the barn and human perspiration, it *is* distinctive. Many Amish are not offended by the smell of sweat and farm; to them it is a natural, earthy smell. I have learned, however, that most Amish are no "dirtier" than their hardworking, English-speaking farm neighbors. Ironically I have listened to one Amishman assert that many of the English houses where he has laid carpet were dirty, demonstrating that lack of cleanliness is not limited to either society.

Another reason why the English are suspicious of the Amish is that they may interact most closely with members who are on the fringes of Amish society. These Amish individuals may have deliberately chosen to work on a carpenter's crew or in a factory (although not all Amish persons who work in such places are on the "fringes") and may have not yet decided not to "join church" and settle down—not yet, or not ever.

Many outsiders do not realize that a child born into an Amish family is not fully "Amish" until he or she takes the vows of membership—which are considered lifetime vows—and hence is not under the direct control of the Amish bishops and ministers. Until he or she makes this crucial choice, an "Amish" youth may dally around with activities that are distinctly un-Amish—and give the community a bad reputation. This fact of Amish life cannot be overly emphasized: too often when outsiders talk about "Amish" youth, they fail to realize the significance of a young person's choice in "joining church" and committing him- or herself to the Amish way of life.

Depending on the youth themselves and the customs of a local area, some "Amish" youth—but by no means all—may own cars, drive them recklessly, and engage in other un-Amish practices. They may ride past English homes in a buggy in the wee hours of the morning with a boom box blaring. Tales of local authorities breaking up late-night drinking parties held in barns by young rebels do nothing to enhance the picture the locals have of the Amish. Of course, the news of the 1998 arrests of two Amish teens for drug dealing, as well as the extreme depictions of Amish waywardness in the documentary *The Devil's Playground,* deny the credibility of the idealistic bucolic scenes described earlier in this chapter.

Like many of our English neighbors, my husband and I held misconceptions about Amish life. Despite the fact that the first house we lived in was built by an Amishman and that we occasionally hired an Amish grandmother to babysit our children, we never truly got to know the Amish as individuals or to understand their culture during the time we lived in Lancaster County. Not that my husband did not try. Gregarious, outgoing, and curious, as well as respectful of Amish culture and beliefs, he tried to get to know them beyond the superficial level.

Finally, through some unusual circumstances, he was introduced to a prominent member of the local Amish community, who then introduced him to some of his friends. When his association with these Amish people became more widely known, other Amish persons assumed that he was trustworthy, and one friendship led to another. This is typical. If an English person gains the confidence of leaders in the community, doors will open—literally—in other Amish settlements as well.

I began accompanying him on his Amish visits, wondering whether my short hair and non-Amish demeanor would be offensive. I discovered, however, that many Amish are willing to overlook such differences and will go beyond polite acceptance to genuine friendship when they know they are accepted and respected for who they are. What I have found is that beyond their plain and simple exteriors are some fascinating human beings.

As my husband and I developed friendships with Amish persons from a wide range of settlements in a number of states, we found that not only do Amish communities differ, but so also do Amish persons within each settlement. Because to the casual observer, the Amish appear to dress and act alike, making it is easy to assume they *are* alike. Of course to some extent this is true: they submit to the constraints of the local church *Ordnung*—that unwritten code of rules that governs the conduct of every church member—whether they agree with all aspects of it or not. The focus of Amish culture is on the community rather than on the individual; they are truly a collectivist society. Therefore, outsiders are tempted to consider them as a monolithic entity rather than as a configuration of human beings with different ways of reacting to and living out the values of their culture.

As I learned more about Amish customs and became acquainted with a growing number of Amish individuals, I began recording my observations about the culture in general and the different ways in which Amish people lived out their values. However, I determined not to write yet another treatise on Amish life declaring, "The Amish do *this*," and "The Amish do *that*." Rather, my aim became to enable readers to "meet" some of the Amish individuals I have met, to experience the settings in which they live, to see them act and hear them speak, and then to think with me about the meaning of their lives and ours—to ponder the practices of our culture as well as Amish culture.

Of course this approach has its limitations. Obviously I cannot reveal Amish society from either the inside out or the outside in, for as John L. Ruth remarks in his video, *The Amish: A People of Preservation*, "Nobody can speak for the Old Order Amish but themselves."[1] Increasingly the Amish, traditionally an oral people, are taking pen—or word processor—in hand to represent themselves. Moreover, the following sketches do not attempt to represent a complete picture of Amish life; instead, they provide glimpses into it. Nor are the individuals depicted "typical" Amish persons any more than the next shopper walking out of the neighborhood supermarket is the "typical" American.

1. *The Amish: A People of Preservation*, rev. ed., written and prod. John L. Ruth, 52 min., Heritage Productions, 1991, videocassette.

Although the chapters portray real persons and situations, some are composites, and in a few cases the order of the events has been altered. Because of the Amish concern for anonymity, at times I have disguised the identities of the characters and changed some of the insignificant details of their backgrounds. However, in all cases the narratives are essentially true. While the majority of the vignettes depict Old Order Amish practices and persons, occasionally I represent those of other plain Anabaptist groups. In these situations I delineate the group or person I am describing.

Here, then, is a patchwork of the images and reflections gleaned from my Amish-watching experiences: glimpses of what it means to be Amish—*and English*—at the beginning of the new millennium. Since we humans are capable of only partially perceiving reality, our images of it are often broken and distorted. Frequently we view the landscape from a limited perspective. Despite our best efforts, always we see through a glass darkly.

∿ 1 ∿

Amish Family Values

Fourteen of us are seated around the supper table in this dimly lit kitchen. My husband and I are guests of this Amish family, a minister and his wife and their ten children. This is our first overnight stay in an Amish home. Four of the younger ones—all boys with blunt haircuts—sit across the table on a wooden bench, their bowed heads in stair-step silhouette against the light from the uncurtained window. At one end of the table are two daughters wearing their white organdy head coverings with narrow untied strings attached. At the other end in a swivel chair sits the father with the baby, a nine-month-old boy in a wooden high chair between him and the mother, with the three-year-old sister on the other side of her. The two oldest sons, young men in their late teens, tanned and muscular from their field work, sit next to my husband and me.

According to Amish custom, the meal begins with silent prayer. Across from me the children sit as motionless as their parents; the only sounds are the ticking of the clock and a few bird calls through the screen door. How do we know when the prayer time is over, I wonder, not wanting to peek lest the children see. Finally the father leans back in his chair, which squeaks slightly, and I know. Sometimes, I learn later, the signal is a gentle sigh.

Daniel, the father, smiles broadly, exposing his white teeth in an expansive welcome. We pass the homemade bread, the Lebanon bologna, the creamed noodles and peas, and the fresh salad made with lettuce gathered from their own garden. We eat in anticipation of the promised dessert, freshly picked strawberries and shortcake.

At times like this, I note, Amish children are truly seen and not heard. They are observers of adult conversation, listening intently in polite silence. Daniel is recalling the recent visit of some members of a Reformed Church from a southern state. I marvel at the interaction, since the ancestors of the Amish were severely persecuted by both Roman Catholics and the Protestant reformers, perhaps even by the ancestors of his Reformed guests. The memory of these persecutions is kept alive by frequent reading from *Martyrs Mirror,* a book containing accounts of people who were tortured and killed for their religious beliefs during the sixteenth and seventeenth centuries.

Daniel relates how his visitors defended the Roman Catholic and Reformed custom of infant baptism, an important issue since the Amish strongly reject this custom. Instead, they practice believers baptism, which normally takes place during the late teenage years as a distinct choice. Baptism is not something that the parents or the church can do alone but requires the full knowledge and consent of the individual, he explains. During the Reformation the groups that rebaptized adults who confessed their faith in Christ were dubbed "Anabaptists," which means "rebaptizers." They are still called that today.

Daniel pauses to butter a slice of bread, folds it, hands it to three-year-old Katie beside him, and continues to explain how his modern-day Reformed visitors had interpreted infant baptism more as dedication, something that must be confirmed later by the children in order to be valid. He is trying to make conversation, I sense—to bridge the gap between the Amish world and ours, his "English" guests. I realize later that the setting is also an indirect catechism class for the listening children.

After we finish our strawberry shortcake, the clatter of plates and tableware stops and the children restrain their wiggling as we bow again for the silent prayer that concludes the meal. This is not the token silent prayer of evangelical custom; instead, we are silent long enough to really pray. I hold my breath, lest I spoil the silence, and listen again for the squeak of Daniel's chair.

Then fifteen-year-old Emma and ten-year-old Rebecca begin clearing the table and washing the dishes while their brothers, Levi, Noah, Reuben, and Benuel (Ben), head for their chores in the barn. Three-year-old Katie rides her scooter in the area between the house and the barn, keeping up with Samuel and James, the brothers nearest her in age. By now the baby, Danny, is asleep in his crib in his parents' bedroom.

As dusk descends, we gather in the sitting area off the kitchen. Containing a simple couch and two rocking chairs, it becomes the center for the evening activities. Daniel and Sarah relax as their children play and tussle on the rug beside them. The children read to themselves and each other, listening to the adult conversation, and occasionally entering in. Surely they must sense they are being watched, not only now but throughout our stay, and undoubtedly are putting on their best behavior. Still, I am impressed.

It is a scene I will find repeated with slight variations in other Amish homes. Sometimes after the evening meal, when the dishes are done, the families will play games at the large kitchen table. In one home the mother plays dominoes with the younger children while the older ones teach me a new version of Monopoly. Since the preschool children speak only Pennsylvania Dutch, a colloquial dialect descended from the German of the Palatinate, communication with them on these occasions is limited to a few English words and lots of smiles. The propane lamp hung from the ceiling casts its arc of light on a circle of security and sharing.

The lack of interference from radio, television, or computer games encourages the children to interact with each other, their parents, and us. I am most fascinated with their satisfaction with simple things. In this house there are no Barbie dolls, Beanie Babies, Legos, Gameboys, video games, busy boxes, or plastic ride-on toys. Instead, a few tractors or trucks, a doll or two, and some dog-eared books are enough; rarely do I hear the children beg for more *things,* although I have heard some beg to be included in an activity. (Later an Amish mother in a different community informed me that her children had Barbie dolls, Beanie Babies, Legos, busy boxes, and ride-on toys and that her children did beg for more *things.* Apparently communities and families differ, but on the whole, Amish children "make do" with fewer material possessions.)

Soon Sarah announces that it is time for the youngest children to go upstairs to bed, and Daniel hunts for the German prayer book from among the Amish magazines and storybooks on the shelf. Though I understand only a few German words and phrases, I catch the sincerity of tone and demeanor. After prayers Sarah shows us to our bedroom by flashlight and demonstrates how to blow out the kerosene light when we are ready for bed.

We are awakened the next morning before daybreak by the harsh, staccato rhythm of the diesel generator located in the barn, signaling that milking time has arrived and the day's work has begun. My husband gropes for his flashlight and watch. "Four forty-three," he groans, leans back on his pillow momentarily, and then lurches out of bed, knowing that if he wants to truly experience Amish life, he must not sleep any later.

During the next few days we observe the interaction of these parents and their children and note how much they value work. Family chores are parceled out according to gender: the girls work in the house and yard and the boys in the barn and fields. This is a well-run household. Sarah is not only mother but also manager, gently directing her children in whatever task is at hand, whether it be preparing for a meal, weeding the garden, or doing the laundry.

Neither she nor her children are overworked. Fifteen-year-old Emma prepares meals very competently, and ten-year-old Rebecca makes "whoopie pies"—sour milk chocolate cookies sandwiched together with a cream filling—with very little supervision. Unbidden she sweeps the kitchen floor after each meal—perhaps because I am present?—taking care not to miss any crumbs. Both girls go about their work without grumbling or rushing their tasks as though they must finish quickly and go on to something else. Yes, I know: they are on their best behavior because of our presence, but they also are contributing to the family's well-being, and the very *doing* of the tasks seems fulfilling for them. Probably they would not verbalize this sense of purpose and belonging, but it is apparent in their demeanor and their quiet unself-conscious confidence.

The secret of the children's attitudes toward work becomes clear in several incidents during our stay. When Sarah asks me to prepare strawberries for supper, I gather the necessary bowls and tools and place them on the kitchen table. As I begin to hull the berries, in comes three-year-old Katie, begging to help. My impulse is to send her away, knowing that her "help" will slow everything down. But Sarah has already lifted her up to the bench and put a plastic bowl in front of her. Placing a berry in her pudgy hand, she shows her how to remove the stem. Katie squashes the berry in the process, then picks up the next berry and tries again. Eventually she learns how. In situations like this, I realize, Amish children are very much both seen and heard.

Out in the barn and the fields my husband experiences the same communal attitude toward work. While in many Amish communities it is now rare for an entire family to work on the farm, this family is fortunate enough to have sufficient means to keep all of their children employed at home—so far. In general, parents prefer to have their offspring work at home where they can learn the value of work while being shielded from outside, "evil" influences. Only after much more contact with Amish families and Amish farms do I understand what Anabaptist historian John L. Ruth meant when he remarked that "the Amish don't farm to live: they live to farm," and that "shared work is, in many cases, the Amishman's recreation."[1]

Daniel and his sons are emptying the cow stalls of manure and spreading it on the fields, and while they do not apologize for the unpleasantness of their task, they excuse my husband from participating. He, however, is eager to enter into all aspects of life on an Amish farm, and so is placed under the tutelage of eleven-year-old Ben who has been driving the mules back and forth from barn to field. Just how skillful and responsible Ben is soon becomes apparent to my husband, who asks if he can try to drive the mules pulling the manure spreader. Only after several unsuccessful attempts does he learn when to signal the mules for a turn into the barn. Daniel and the visiting veterinarian have a good laugh about how my husband is probably the only college professor in the state forking manure this bright June morning.

When the six-year-old neglects his task of sweeping out the forebay in the barn, his ten-year-old sister offers to help, but he resists. The father speaks to him softly but firmly in Pennsylvania Dutch, and immediately he is trudging out, broom in hand. Both parents assert that learning to work is essential for children long before they go to school. Sarah remarks to us that the local schoolteacher has commented that she knows which children are accustomed to working by the way in which they attack their schoolwork.

Later Sarah, the older girls, and I scrub down the inside of the section of the barn where the cows are milked, in preparation for the coming Sunday when worship services will be held at their farm. I wonder about the necessity of washing down the cow parlor since the services will either be held in the house or another part of the barn.

As we progress along the milking stalls, we are joined by Katie and James, who beg to help. Again I find myself wanting to shoo them out to play, but Sarah never hesitates. Reaching for a bucket, she explains to Katie how to wash down the walls while sending James for the hose. Of course we and they end up much wetter than we would have without their assistance, but Sarah appears not even to consider the matter.

1. John L. Ruth, Elderhostel: "Pennsylvania Dutch Culture," Spruce Lake Retreat, Canadensis, Pa., June 2–7, 2002.

Her unintended lesson is not lost on me: while they are very young the children must learn to be contributing members of the family and the community. If, as has been suggested, two primary goals for humans to achieve are the abilities to love and to work, then the Amish are in the forefront in helping their offspring develop those traits.

But the Amish also teach their children another important lesson that is increasingly neglected in English society: to respect and submit to authority. From the experiences of an acquaintance who also spent some time in an Amish home, I know that the quietness of the children during prayer times before and after meals comes only through deliberate discipline by parents. She observed the efforts of a mother and father who expected their fifteen-month-old child not to fuss during prayer time, and when he did, they waited until he complied. Not only do Amish children learn to work and to love, but they also learn to obey.

This and much more I absorb from our first stay with this Amish family. What I do not know is how important they will become in my life, even though we are separated by over an hour's drive—and by disparities in culture. We will return again and again to learn from them, counting them among our most admired friends. We will bring our own sons and our friends to visit, sensing that the wisdom of living that our Amish friends embody in many ways surpasses the wisdom of books and degrees.

꙳ 2 ꙳

Three Long Hours of Sitting Still

The scattered horse droppings and carriage wheel tracks on the pavement reassure me I am headed in the right direction for this summer morning's Amish church service. Held on alternate Sundays in the homes or barns of members of each district, the Amish church service is a central feature of community life. Although the deacon couple at whose home the service will be conducted have invited my husband and me to attend, we have stayed overnight with another family a few miles away. My husband has preceded me, having left an hour earlier with our host and hostess in their carriage.

I drive past enclaves of houses, barns, and sheds surrounded by tidy gardens and broad fields, their legendary Amish neatness shimmering in the June sunshine. The carriage tracks turn sharply into a lane, and clusters of gray carriages in front of the farmhouse come into view. My husband's light-blue shirt stands out clearly against the mass of white long-sleeved shirts, black vests and pants, and straw hats. The horses are already quartered in their stalls or tethered under trees. On this warm June morning I note thankfully that the service will be held in the cool basement of the house.

Having previously attended Amish worship services in several settlements, I am familiar with the rituals that are a part of them. Prior to the service, members of the community assemble by age and sex in specially designated areas. The men somberly shake hands with the men, the women with the women, and the men and ministers greet each other with a "holy kiss," a custom practiced in most Amish communities. In some settlements, the women do this as well. Generally the preservice talking is subdued and sporadic.

Dressed in a blue cotton skirt and white blouse, wearing no makeup and no jewelry except my wedding ring, I join the older women attired in black or dark-colored dresses already seated on plain wooden benches in a corner of the basement. I protest inwardly, "I'm not that old!" Later I realize this is actually a compliment, since they are treating me with the respect reserved for older people in the Amish community.

Soon the younger women enter, several holding babies and some with a toddler or two in tow. Next the older children and the teenage girls process down the basement stairs, silently sliding onto the benches assigned to them, as directed by the woman at whose home the service is being held. Then the bishop, ministers, and deacon enter through a side door, followed by the adult men, some holding children or leading them by the hand. Lastly come the teenage boys with averted eyes, shaking hands with the ministers as they pass through their ranks.

When everyone is seated (close to two hundred of us) the men and boys remove their hats virtually in unison and place them on nails attached to the joists above them or under the benches, except for the ministers who keep theirs on until the first song begins. Few worshipers talk or smile, denoting the seriousness of the occasion. As the somber strains of the first hymn break the summer morning stillness, the ministers, who are seated facing each other on chairs near the center of the assemblage, rise and file out, hats in hand. They will consult each other about aspects of the service before returning.

The congregation sings in unison, as always, ponderously wandering up and down among several notes for each syllable, reminding me of a cross between a bagpipe's drone and a funeral dirge. This morning the congregation sings more heartily than usual, although I note that not a single teenager, male or female, joins in. Some of the *Vorsangers,* the male singers who begin the first syllable of each line in solo, are quite skilled in the convoluted musical patterns; others seem unsure of themselves, and the singing falters on several occasions.

An Amish hymn—or the four or five verses of one which are sung—may last twenty or thirty minutes. The particular hymns and the scripture for each Sunday of the year follow a set schedule. The second hymn, the "Lob Lied" (praise song), is sung every Sunday in Old Order Amish services without exception. This morning we sing a third hymn and then a fourth one, waiting for the return of the ministers, who are deciding, among other things, which of the visiting ministers will bring the main sermon this morning. Usually the one with the longest tenure is chosen. When they return, we finish the verse we have begun, and the designated minister rises and speaks in a combination of High German and Pennsylvania Dutch. This is known as the "short sermon," which will continue for about a half hour.

With downcast eyes and quavering voice, the first speaker stands and faces the congregation, and without benefit of pulpit, table, or notes, delivers his singsong homily. He does not look at his listeners, nor do they look at him. Only after attending several services have I realized that the avoidance of eye contact may signal humility on the part of the speaker who feels that he is unworthy of the message he is delivering. The listeners bow their heads, perhaps in deference to those under whose authority they have been placed—and perhaps, according to one Amishman, because they are contemplating the seriousness of the message. Other visits to Amish church services confirm that Amish preachers in general do not follow some of the rules of public speaking considered essential by so-called authorities on communication.

Trying to take as little space on the bench as possible, I hunch my shoulders and scrunch down in an attempt to blend inconspicuously into the congregation. Furtively I observe the worshipers around me. Most of the preadolescent girls are watching my every move. Noting that the women beside me do not cross their legs at the knee, only at the ankle, I try to imitate them. Forty-five minutes into the service I give up and cross my legs at the knee. I begin to appreciate an Amish friend's observation that one reason why Amish men make good bow hunters is that they have developed the necessary patience by quietly sitting through three-hour church services.

Two worshipers arrive late, a teenage girl and boy. The deacon's wife directs both of them to their places on the respective benches for their age groups, and both immediately bow their heads and keep them bowed until after the prayer and scripture. Since many of the other teenagers sit with bowed heads, I cannot tell whether their actions represent embarrassment or guilt, or whether they are merely an exaggeration of the behavior of their friends. Perhaps they are late because they have met with the ministers during the earlier part of the service to receive instruction prior to becoming members. Such classes last for approximately nine sessions.

This settlement has a reputation for the wayward behavior of some of its youth, but to the casual observer, nothing in the dress or demeanor of the young people this morning would suggest anything less than full compliance. The teen girls' neat dresses are predominantly in shades of blue or purple, and their white organdy aprons are precisely pinned over them. They wear either white or black head coverings, and a few are dressed in the black of mourning. However, subtle clues to their lack of compliance with Amish standards are evident in the stylishness of their shoes and the snugness of their dresses.

The teenage boys all wear white shirts, some obviously homemade, others store-bought. Their black vests and pants make them look quite dapper, and none of the haircuts are of the Dutch-boy or "bowl" variety. Several show a precision and style that probably was achieved in a salon or first-class barbershop. Since both places are "off-limits" for Amish persons, such haircuts may connote rebellion.

I wonder where the youth were last night—whether there was a "band hop" in someone's barn. Are they aware that the deacon's wife, who so primly directed them to their seats this morning, was three months' pregnant on her wedding day? The birth of her child—plainly recorded on the plaque on the wall upstairs in her sitting room—took place only six months after her marriage. Stepping out of line in petty and more serious ways is not limited to this generation of Amish youth.

The short sermon ends abruptly, and the congregation rises and turns around, falling to their knees so quickly that I can scarcely follow. We kneel at our benches for several minutes of silent prayer followed by a prayer by one of the ministers. Next we rise and face the back while the deacon reads the prescribed scripture in High German. Typically, this time is an unofficial bathroom break during which some of the teenage males hike off to the barn and young mothers trot their little ones up the stairs of the house.

After the Bible reading, a visiting minister commences what colloquially is dubbed the "long sermon," which everyone assumes will last at least an hour. I settle in for the duration, since I know only a few words of Pennsylvania Dutch and none of German. Occasionally—more often in a New Order Amish service—the minister may slip in a bit of English for the benefit of his non-Amish guests, quoting a verse of scripture or a few words and phrases that are crucial to the morning message. But since this is an Old Order service, this morning's sermon is rendered entirely in a blend of German and Pennsylvania Dutch.

The visiting minister has come from a neighboring district, having ridden across the valley for more than two hours in order to attend. His own district does not have service this morning; this is their "home" Sunday, the alternate Sunday set apart for visiting family and friends.

His style is different from that of any Amish minister I have watched before. He paces back and forth in front of the assemblage, speaking in less of a singsong manner than usual. Now and then his voice breaks, and on several occasions he looks directly at the youth in the congregation as though admonishing them. Amish ministers are not afraid to show their emotions; frequently they cry as they preach, yet they still deliver their message firmly. I tire of analyzing his style and try to meditate, knowing that God is not limited to my understanding of the exact content of the service. I can catch the tone and the spirit of worship, regardless of the language barrier and the cultural constraints.

But this morning I am distracted from my meditations because of my curiosity concerning the interaction of the parents and children sitting around me. The youngest ones, toddlers to nine-year-olds, sit with a parent, mostly the little girls with their mothers and the little boys with their fathers, but not always. Sometimes the father will take the baby for a while, bottle and all, or a grandmother will tend the grandchild by her side. Throughout the service mothers and smaller children move in and out, taking trips to the upstairs bathroom or to one of the bedrooms that they use as a nursery. A child may slip shyly through the rows of benches to the other parent or the grandmother, guided along the way by hand motions.

Dressed in their Sunday clothes, the children sit quietly with little squirming and no whispering. Attired in plain, mostly dark-colored dresses topped with white organdy pinafores reserved for Sundays, the little girls wear white heart-shaped organdy coverings over their hair, which is parted in the middle and tightly drawn back. The little boys look like miniatures of their fathers and older brothers, wearing black vests and pants and straw hats. Every Amish boy from the age of three or so is encouraged by his parents to wear his hat when he goes outside. Sociologically this is a sound practice; it sets the Amish boys off as separate from mainstream society as emphatically as the coverings and cape dresses distinguish the girls.

How do they keep the toddlers so quiet, I marvel, as I have marveled in every Amish service I have attended. Only the infants cry or fuss—even the older babies rarely cry. Never have I seen any evidence of stern discipline; only once have I observed any kind of physical restraint, and that was fairly mild. In response to the excessive squirming of her three-year-old daughter, the mother—without any apparent sign of anger—deliberately grasped her shoulders firmly and set her on the bench beside her. The little girl whimpered for a brief moment, which the mother ignored, and then settled down quietly. Sometimes simple toys, such as plastic keys or rings on a chain, will be given to the smallest toddlers. This morning I watch two of the little ones, a boy and girl, studiously fold and unfold pocket handkerchiefs.

More careful observation, however, reveals one of the secrets: the subtle manner in which Amish parents signal to their children the imperative of silence. Unlike many English mothers who hold their older babies and toddlers on their laps and interact with them through smiles, pats, gentle motions, and whispers, Amish parents' body language signals that this is no time for communication. They avoid eye contact, speaking, or smiling, and they frown at any talking. I note, though, that both fathers and mothers gently hug and caress the little ones in their arms.

The Amish way of handling children in worship services contrasts significantly with that of English parents in many mainstream churches. Weary of a child's noisy and disobedient clamoring, an English parent sometimes may impulsively scoop the child up in his or her arms and stomp out, treating the captive congregation to the sounds of a spanking, punctuated by sharp words and the child's angry wails. The other extreme is represented by the permissiveness of one adoring mother at a Wednesday Bible study. She seemed to think that everyone around her child should adapt to his moods and allowed the little boy to run noisily back and forth in the room and the adjoining hall, chattering excitedly.

Mostly, however, children are removed from worship services in mainstream churches. If they are present at all, they are hurried away after the second hymn or the children's "sermon." One highly respected authority among evangelicals asserts that two-year-olds should not be present at public worship services—even if this requires hiring babysitters to keep them at home—since they are incapable of sitting still. Obviously he has never attended an Amish worship service. His beliefs regarding what should be expected of small children are strikingly different from those expressed in letters to the editor in the Amish publication *Family Life*. One writer insists that "8 10 month old babies are not too young to keep . . . seated on your lap" and that "babies of any age should not stand on mother's lap and watch the children behind him." The writer adds that she feels "this is a tender age where much can be learned by attending church and listening." She concludes that "if 10-month-olds should sit quietly why not 10-year olds!"[1]

Surreptitiously I glance at my watch, calculating that I must endure at least twenty minutes more of a sermon I cannot understand, so I study the rows of people around me. No one seems to be focused on the minister, but then not many people appear to be sleeping either, although the measured breathing and telltale wheezes from the bench behind me suggest that somebody is. Three hours of sitting silent and still is a long time. But then I am not accustomed to the slow and deliberate cadences of the Amish life, the unhurried tempo, the sense that there is nowhere better to go and nothing more important to do. Finally I smell the odors of a lighted match and propane gas and assume that the sermon must be nearing its conclusion. Someone has started heating water for coffee.

After the minister has completed his hour's labor, two ministers and a deacon "bear witness" to the truth of what he has said, speaking from their seats. The first minister talks for about ten minutes, wiping his eyes several times as he speaks, and the second minister and the deacon follow with briefer but earnest comments. Then come the final hymn and the closing prayer, during which each person genuflects slightly at the name of Jesus, reminiscent of the Roman Catholic custom. The early Anabaptists considered themselves neither Catholic nor Protestant, and if asked about this, many Anabaptists today would concur.

After the service, I watch as the men quickly transform the benches into tables and cover them with paper tablecloths, and the host family and their relatives immediately set them with cups and saucers and knives. The women spread out the food that is standard fare for every postservice meal in this settlement: homemade bread and/or store-bought bread, cold meats, and sliced cheese, cup cheese, pickles, and pickled red beets. They set out butter and a spread consisting of a mixture of honey and peanut butter for the bread. With such a rigidly prescribed menu, hosting families are less likely to feel competitive; the uniformity results in a leveling that very effectively reduces the temptation for show or status as surely as the dress code does.

As guests, we are invited to share this light lunch with the first "sitting," consisting of the older men and women and some of the smaller

1. Also a mother in Ontario, "Letters to the Editor: Taking Notes in Church," *Family Life*, Nov. 1986, 4.

children. The younger men and women will eat when we are finished, and possibly a third sitting will be necessary for the teenagers and older children. However, some of the teenagers—especially the males—choose not to wait for their turn, but instead hurry out to harness their horses and are soon clip-clopping away in their carriages.

Everyone, whether eating at this setting or not, pauses for the silent prayer that begins all Amish meals. We use our saucers as plates, and place our cups on the tablecloth beside them. By observing the other women at my table I see how to manipulate my knife to remove the meats and the pickles from their trays, and someone remarks lightly that I am learning fast. Our hostess and her relatives move about serving coffee and hot mint tea, known locally as "meadow tea," as well as pieces of homemade apple and *Schnitz* (dried apple) pie. When everyone has eaten we bow again for silent prayer, and the women remove the dishes and wash them for the second setting.

After the meal the assemblage gradually disbands and parents gather children from house and yard and barn where they have been playing with friends. Often relatives and friends are invited to stay for the afternoon and have supper with the host family, but when we are invited to stay, my husband regretfully declines the invitation.

We have sat on hard benches through a three-hour service conducted in a language we cannot understand. We have learned that for the Amish the church is people, not place; that worship is communal rather than individual; that order, structure, ritual, and tradition provide boundaries for channeling faith and life and giving them stability and meaning. We perceive that simplicity and plainness have a beauty of their own.

Moreover, the simple sameness of setting and program as well as the careful adherence to established patterns—worshiping in a crude barn or shop and sharing a standardized meal—serve as deterrents to the competitive and prideful seeking after status that fosters discontent and division. Within the simple, traditional, communal style of worship the individual can find his or her place. Children learn the beliefs and practices of the community by observation and participation; at an early age they are expected to take their places as parts of the whole.

Other parts of the rituals function in both symbolic and practical ways. The exclusive use of Pennsylvania Dutch and German serves as a reminder to the members of the community that they are not a part of the outside world but are separated unto God. This language barrier also makes it hard for outsiders to intrude upon their worship. (Unfortunately, High German can also become a barrier to their own youth's understanding.) And the choice of unison rather than harmonic singing stresses the importance of unity among the members. Also, the custom of having multiple ministers rather than one lessens the danger of any of them feeling too much of a sense of power or responsibility in his position. Because the ministers have been chosen by lot, and because they sit and preach from the same level as the people to whom they minister rather than from a raised platform, they are reminded that they are not above the congregation but a part of it.

But this morning the emphasis on family stands out more clearly to me than any of the other facets. Sometimes the programs of churches foster the fragmentation of the family rather than encourage its unity. Often the generations cannot even worship together because they respond only to their preferred musical "languages" and worship styles. The Amish unity contrasts to this gap between the generations, perhaps largely because children from their earliest years on are a part of the traditional worship practices.

Many child advocates would object to requiring little children to sit still through three-hour services. Some might even label these expectations as abusive. They do not seem abused—these children who are cuddled, hugged, and cherished but who also are expected to obey. Could they be stronger for having been given boundaries and for having been taught that they can control their impulses for the betterment of both themselves and the communities to which they belong? The Amish would contend that they may learn more quickly, that they are not the center of the universe, but that God is. And for them, this is perhaps the most important lesson of all.

~: 3 :~

Countercultural Ideals

O LORD, my heart is not lifted up,
my eyes are not raised too high;
I do not occupy myself with things
too great and too marvelous for me.
But I have calmed and quieted my soul,
like a child quieted at its mother's breast;
like a child that is quieted is my soul.
(Psalm 131: 1–2, RSV)

G*elassenheit* is the German word for the quintessential Amish ideal much touted by students of Amish society, but it is a term rarely used by the Amish themselves. Gelassenheit is defined as yielding to God and his will and submitting to the community as well. It is demonstrated by humble acceptance of one's role and state in life—by not thinking of oneself more highly than one ought. Indeed, it often means not thinking of oneself at all, but instead considering the needs of others and respecting their opinions as much, and perhaps more, than one's own. This quality is directly opposed to the self-centered values of mainstream American society, with its emphasis on self-esteem, self-fulfillment, self-assertion, and self-actualization.

Strangely, I think of Gelassenheit when I come across a particular magazine ad for milk. As I turn the page, a shorthaired woman dressed in a scarlet bathing suit—a celebrity, of course—stares at me with arrogant, sultry eyes and a come-hither look. Not that scarlet clothing, sultry eyes, and come-hither looks are new, but the sharp sense of distaste I experience inspires a contrasting picture—that of wide-eyed, somberly dressed children peering through the back opening of an Amish carriage or the organdy halos adorning young Amish mothers cradling babies or tending toddlers. Of course the halos are only an illusion, and the somber Amish clothing cloaks the entire spectrum of transgressions of which humankind is guilty. Amish sins are a fact of life as much as those committed by scarlet women, but at least the Amish aren't so brazen about it. They know they are sinners. Or I should say, to the extent that they comprehend the spirit of Gelassenheit, they know.

My introduction to Gelassenheit came when I observed the way the Amish and other Anabaptists phrased their statements. Rather than the dogmatic assertions I heard thundered by the camp meeting preachers of my childhood, which were often punctuated by fists banging on hard wooden pulpits, the conjectures of many Amish I met began or ended tentatively with the softly spoken phrase, "I believe." The accompanying body language was nonassertive and nonthreatening.

What I initially failed to realize was that convictions expressed in this manner can be firmly held, even though they usually are not flaunted in ways that irritate or alienate. In addition, while the spirit of the speaker demonstrates his or her willingness to listen, the noncommittal body language displayed at that point leaves the English speaker wondering whether, in fact, he or she has truly been heard. Probably largely because of this nonassertive and even hesitant conversational style, the Amish are sometimes thought of as "dumb Dutchmen." Even their English neighbors fail to understand that the Amish style is not to confront or flaunt, or that often their silence does not represent stupidity, but rather humility and a polite respect for other human beings with whom they may disagree.

Another facet of Gelassenheit was aptly demonstrated by Amish friends of ours when the husband was chosen to be a bishop, a position of high regard in the Amish community. However, since the persons filling those positions are chosen by lot and thought to be appointed by God, most ministers and bishops approach their new tasks with feelings of unworthiness and a sense of the weightiness of their responsibilities. When we visited our friends soon after the appointment, my husband remarked that he didn't think congratulations were appropriate, and his wife concurred. We discovered that many of the members of the district had been visiting them, offering support, but from the solemn manner in which our friends related this, we had the sense that these were occasions of the giving and receiving of condolences.

One intriguing aspect of Gelassenheit is that it does not appear to result in a lack of self-esteem. Of course, self-esteem is not thought about much in Amish society. Instead, the Amish stress the more biblical quality of self-sacrifice, which shifts the focus away from the abstract to the practical. Jesus never talked about self-esteem, although his treatment of people on all levels of society demonstrated that they had value. He modeled an outward rather than an inward focus, which is also characteristic of Gelassenheit.

This self-forgetfulness is evident in the way Amish children learn early to blend in rather than to stand out and to contribute to the well-being of the family and community. Parents rarely have to invent tasks, such as taking out the garbage, for children in Amish homes. Young boys learn to harness the horse and lead him to the buggy, saving their fathers some time. Girls learn to cook and to bake for the family when they are quite young; I once watched a fifteen-year-old girl prepare a complete meal. More often the females in the family work together. A sense of competency and of contributing to the general good replaces the goal of being number one. These accomplishments, of course, are much more attainable.

An example of their choosing to be nonassertive is illustrated by an Amish businessman's refusal to prosecute many of his clients who are in arrears in accounts payable, making the total he is owed in the thousands. When asked whether he might consider bringing suit to gain that which is rightfully his, his reply was, "If they can live with themselves knowing what they have done, that's their problem. I'm not going to lose any sleep over it." Showing no sign of bitterness, he remarked that he would go into another line of business rather than take legal action. In a subsequent conversation, he quoted with conviction the Apostle Paul's declaration that "godliness with contentment is great gain" (I Timothy 6:6, NIV), a verse that both his actions and demeanor illustrate.

While humility and the absence of self-assertiveness are the first aspects of Gelassenheit that I encountered, I have since come to realize that submission is also basic to the working out of Gelassenheit in Amish lives. Again, this quality stands in direct opposition to mainstream American culture. The illusion that we have control over our lives is fundamental to American social and political doctrine. Asserted clearly in our Declaration of Independence, the right to "life, liberty, and the pursuit of happiness" forms the bedrock on which not only our Constitution, but also our social system operates. Individual freedoms are paramount. It is our manifest destiny to control the patterns of our lives. We resent interference from any force or authority that attempts to usurp our preeminent position.

Nobody is going to tell us what to do with our bodies, our money, our time, our children—not the government, not our parents, certainly not a church, and, very often, not even God.

This is in direct contrast to the Amish point of view. While few Amish know the term Gelassenheit, and many do not even think about such concepts, they live in a society where the lifestyle leads them to a practical understanding of it. Most of them bend to the will of the community, respect the authority of parents and elders, and submit to government and law unless these policies come into conflict with their interpretation of the Bible. They attempt to live out the will of God in their lives according to the community's understanding of scripture.

The spirit of Gelassenheit involves submission to the Ordnung of the district—that unwritten but generally understood code of conduct covering many of the activities of daily life. It even deals with such minutiae as the position of a pleat on a prayer covering and the content of the periodicals in the magazine rack, as well as the kinds of machinery found in the barn and the field. It explains why a couple will move into a newly purchased house and remove the electrical wires, the phones, the lightning rod, and even the indoor-outdoor carpet on the porch. While the specific requirements will vary from settlement to settlement—some districts will require only that the electricity not be used rather than be torn out—the real issue is whether the person is willing to submit to the authority of the district's Ordnung.

Gelassenheit is demonstrated by one Amishman who was once very active in a local historical society but who has since withdrawn his membership. His bishop determined that his involvement not only placed him in too close contact with outsiders but also gave him too much public attention. Another Amishman has discontinued his writing activities— even though they were religious and educational in nature—because they came into conflict with the desires of the local church district.

Still another Amishman has given up his lucrative motor repair business and moved his family across the state to a more conservative settlement. He did this, he confesses, partly because he came to realize that some of the activities he carried out surreptitiously to maintain his business were in violation of the district's Ordnung and marked him as a hypocrite. It was also partly because he felt the influences on his growing family in the new settlement would be more conducive to their embracing the Amish way of life.

Another example of this submission is the way the Amish accept the events of their lives, whether pleasant or painful, as coming from the hand of God. This acceptance of one's lot in life is best illustrated by the manner in which most Amish deal with life's tragedies and vicissitudes. They spend much less time than Christians from most other groups questioning why the child was killed in a car-carriage accident, why a family member has suffered from and then been lost to cancer, or why a baby is born with Down's syndrome, dwarfism, or some handicap. In the newspapers that circulate in the Amish communities—*The Budget, Die Botschaft,* and *The Diary*—the report of an unexpected death by the local "scribe" often includes a line such as "We don't understand why God chose to take her now, but we know that we shouldn't question His will even though we will miss her more than we can say. God makes no mistakes." Among the Amish is a strong sense that heaven is a better place, that God will not give a person more than that person can bear, and that God can bring good out of the tragedies in their lives.

Of course the Amish slip from their ideal of Gelassenheit. Church splits, power struggles, and family dissensions caused by pride mar their society as well as our own. Gelassenheit is, however, a virtue they keep working to attain.

And we English would be more truthful if we admitted that regardless of our emphasis on directing our own destinies, many events in our lives are ultimately beyond our control. Despite our attempts to be the right person in the right place doing the right thing at the right time, advancement passes us by. Despite good genes, excellent prenatal care, and skilled medical attention, we give birth to developmentally and physically disabled children. Vehicles and business ventures crash alike for the just and the unjust, the prepared and the unprepared, the English as well as the Amish. Perhaps, however, the Amish are under fewer delusions concerning the amount of control they have. Perhaps also their unsystematic but practical theology helps them to cope better when, as Ecclesiastes 12:6 declares, the wheel loosens, the pitcher shatters, the silver cord snaps, the golden bowl is broken. They agree with the writer of Ecclesiastes who determines later in the chapter that "the conclusion of the matter" is to "fear God and keep his commandments, for this is the whole duty of man" (12:13b, NIV).

❦ 4 ❧

An Amish Intellectual

"Did you see the recent television special on the Amish?" the voice on the phone queries after only a brief exchange of pleasantries involving weather and family well-being. He is referring to a recent television presentation that focused on some sensational cases of child abuse and psychological coercion that placed an entire Amish community in a negative light.[1] Those Amish persons who take seriously the constraints of their local Ordnung rarely if ever view television programs, but they will bend the rules if the occasion warrants it. The man on the other end of the line is dedicated to his way of life, sincere and devout. I hesitate, then decide not to ask whether he watched it. Somehow he has learned about the negative content of the program and is not pleased with it.

I reply that we had seen the program, wondering what he will ask next. One of the first Amish persons my husband and I came to know on more than a superficial level, Reuben is often more adept at evaluating our way of life than we are at understanding his.

"What did you think of it?" His voice is as slow and deliberate as always, but this time I sense a slight edge to his tone. He wants me not to approve of the program.

My husband first encountered him as he stood beside a display of coal stoves in the center of a walkway at one of the largest shopping malls in the area. Curious about the stoves—as well as the man who was selling them—my husband engaged him in conversation, fascinated by the contrast between the man and his wares and the glitzy ambience of the mall. A diminutive figure dressed in Amish black and wearing the predictable broad-brimmed hat, he carried himself with poise and assurance, answering questions about the stoves with the ease and definiteness that comes with a sure knowledge. He was indeed convincing: we later bought a stove, which he installed and serviced and which became our primary source of heat for a number of years.

That was over twenty years ago. Now his family has expanded from

1. "The Secret of the Amish," ABC's 20/20, aired Feb. 21 and July 25, 1997.

one son to seven children, and he has built an attractive addition to their solid brick farmhouse. Along the way he has undertaken various financial enterprises in addition to selling and servicing European-style coal and wood stoves. Since produce farming has been his main source of income, he has experimented with hydroponic farming methods, specifically with tomatoes and strawberries. For several years he bred llamas in an attempt to cash in on a hikers' fad of using them as pack animals. He also is a widely known tax accountant in the Amish community. And he was chosen to be a minister and later a bishop, both unpaid vocations in the Amish community but which involve much responsibility and command great respect.

My husband still remembers their first conversation as indicative of Reuben's personality and interests. Upon learning that he liked to read, my husband questioned him concerning his favorite reading material. Expecting his response to be *Martyrs Mirror* or the local Amish newspaper, my husband was surprised when Reuben replied that recently he had been reading books on economics.

"Why economics?" my husband inquired.

Always reticent, Reuben thought for a moment and then quietly responded that since our economy was undergoing a period of inflation, he wanted to find out more about the causes of inflation. Drawing him out, my husband discovered that he had taught school in a nearby county, which is unusual for an Amish male in Pennsylvania, that his wife had also been a schoolteacher before their marriage, and that years later both of them had taken a speed-reading course, during which they had read George Orwell's *Animal Farm*.

Not your typical Amishman, my husband decided. Of course he since has learned that a "typical" Amish person does not exist. Still, Reuben is unusual in that he is more perceptive than most human beings, English or Amish, and I often find myself challenged by his intellect. His education has obviously not terminated with his eight years of formal schooling.

On one occasion when he was servicing our stove, I arrived home fresh from a session with my Literature and the Environment class. During the supper we shared afterward, my husband referred to my course, and Reuben was immediately curious regarding its content. I explained a little about what I was teaching as well as my goals for the semester, and he nodded with understanding. He sat for a minute stirring his soup and then asked whether I had challenged my students to consider the teleological aspects of Charles Darwin's *The Origin of Species*.

Despite his quiet, unassuming demeanor, Reuben demonstrates remarkable ability to communicate to groups as well as individuals. He has been a speaker on at least two occasions to assemblages at a local college. Once he addressed the behavioral science department at a dinner, and another time he served on a panel with a lawyer and a businessman, speaking to a group of over 250 students on lifestyle issues. A professor who attended the session remarked afterward that his was easily the most organized and articulate presentation of the three. And a minister colleague of his confided to my husband that his own children listened with rapt attention to a sermon by Reuben which recounted Anabaptist history.

He is tired of all the books and articles on the Amish, he once asserted, exhibiting the desire of most Amish to be left alone to live their way of life in peace. It is a lifestyle in which he was not only nurtured but also which he has examined and chosen; he would concur with Socrates that the unexamined life is not worth living, and he would understand what Socrates meant in other passages, if he were motivated to read him. He doesn't say it, but I sense that he is weary of being treated as though he and his kind are animals on exhibit in a zoo, a display that he points out nets millions of dollars in revenue from tourists in the larger settlements of Lancaster County, Pennsylvania; Elkhart and LaGrange counties, Indiana; and Holmes County, Ohio. But since his curiosity is stronger than his irritation, he can't resist reading what is being written about his people. Sometimes he responds in writing himself. When he does, the average reader may find it difficult to discern that the critique has not been drafted by a person with advanced degrees. *Plain and Amish: An Alternative to Modern Pessimism* by Bernd G. Langin inspired a response from Reuben, which was published in a state historical magazine.[2] In his review, Reuben assesses Langin's level of accuracy in evaluating Amish culture: "Langin does not see the Amish as a cult. This is a theocentric culture, reminiscent of medieval times, which has survived the philosophy of humanism. The Amish are Anabaptist and they know it." Reuben also notes Langin's honesty and realism, "However, as a zealot for good journalism, Langin does not

---

2. Review of *Plain and Amish: An Alternative to Modern Pessimism,* by Bernd G. Langin, *Pennsylvania Mennonite Heritage* 19 (Apr. 1996): 37.

allow us to stereotype Anabaptism as perfect innocence and godliness. He exposes those early Anabaptists who endorsed communism, polygamy, and taking up arms against humans and governments. Their persecution of Anabaptists was not totally without warrant."

He appreciates Langin's sensitivity to the logic behind many Amish customs, and as he evaluates the book, his own conviction regarding the benefits of Amish life comes through when he writes,

> Horse and buggy travel is not seen as a handicap. The Amish are forced to travel wisely; a taxi may be hired if necessary. Businesses start small. By design they fill a niche that large corporations over-look or cannot fill. Electronic marvels are rivaled by creative mechanical ingenuity and a dedicated work ethic. . . . As for schooling, victims of today's corporate downsizing are acutely aware that job security is not an automatic adjunct to a degree.

But he is piqued by what he deems an unnecessary emphasis on sexual matters in Langin's writing:

> Today's media saturates readers with sexual images, but one hardly expects this in a book on the Amish. Perhaps all journalists are plagued with the scourge of eros-myopia. Do the Amish men in Allen County think their women are the most beautiful in the world? Does the outside world go after Amish women? Do Amish teen-aged girls possess the most innocent sex appeal that Langin has ever seen? This is hard to believe!

During our phone conversation about the 20/20 television program on the Amish, he expresses his exasperation with the presentation that focused on sexual abuse, the physical abuse of children, and the psychological effects of shunning. He has written a letter to the program's producers. Would we want to read a copy?

Of course we would, I respond. We too were dismayed by the program, fearing that the viewing audience would generalize from the examples of a few very slanted cases to assume that such behavior is typical of Amish culture. The program could lead many viewers who see the Amish only in bucolic photographs in coffee-table books to conclude that they are hypocrites.

He does not want people staring at him as he walks down the street and looking down on him because they assume he is guilty of such deeds, he declares. Later my husband expresses surprise at his sensitivity. Amish are not supposed to care what "the world" says about them; to have onlookers "falsely say all kinds of evil against you because of me" (Matthew 5:11, NIV) is a part of the price of separation from the world. But his is a very natural response: to be looked down upon because one embraces the values of plainness, simplicity, and clean living is tolerable, but to be ostracized because one is falsely accused of acts that directly contradict those values is hard to take.

It is for these reasons that Reuben has chosen to write. In his four-page, single-spaced, typed letter he expresses his frustration and his weariness with the media's sensationalism, especially the "snippets that exploit the Amish people and culture." He observes,

> With perfect aplomb, the reporter tells us that 20/20's search for truth has revealed a dark side of Amish culture that heretofore has been hidden behind a facade of quaint, pastoral tranquility. And now, for the first time in the history of journalism, the true, correct, and completely honest account of Amish culture has finally been revealed for all the world to see: Amish bishops rule with an arbitrary, iron-fisted, and totalitarian control, which leaves their constituency with no meaningful choices in life; and Amish parents habitually abuse their children.

In the letter he defends his culture with descriptors that outsiders who know the Amish most intimately would themselves employ:

> The Amish are neither all good, nor are they all bad. But they have much to offer by their example of self-discipline, a quality work ethic, acts of charity, and a warm, honest compassion. . . . To various degrees, all communities and cultures are plagued with the so-called dregs of society, and the Amish are no exception. But, if I had to choose a new next-door neighbor from the worst of the worst out of an Amish community, or from the worst of the worst out of society at large, the oddity from the Amish community would win hands down. All his faults and quirks and idiosyncrasies seem benign in comparison.

Many English neighbors of Amish would agree with him. At the least, the Amish mostly mind their own business; perhaps their most irritating behaviors are bothering their neighbors for car rides, asking to use the telephone, or slowing down traffic with their horses and carriages. But when misfortune strikes, such as a fire or flood, a contingency of Amish persons are soon on hand to help out; whether the suffering family is Amish or English does not matter. Finally, toward the end of his letter Reuben reveals his identity, stating,

> I have always been Amish. I am middle-aged and happily married to a beautiful and intelligent woman. We have been blessed with a wonderful family of 7 children. Throughout the 43 years of my life myriads of choices have drifted in and out of my consciousness to sing their sirens of promise. Today, I am cognizant of more choices within my grasp, whether vocational, intellectual, spiritual, or other, than I could possibly live and enjoy in a dozen lifetimes. But, I am happy and contented and fulfilled right here. I am not deprived, for life has been good to me.

His writing is commendable in a culture that is primarily oral. But in a true sense the culture is not so much oral as it is practical—the Amish express their faith in their manner of living rather than in words. What 20/20 failed to acknowledge was the multitude of Amish persons, who, like Reuben, thoughtfully live out their faith with such integrity that mainstream Americans cannot write them off—or leave them alone.

~ 5 ~

A Wedding and a Wedding Tale

"No, I don't think you should do a chapter on an Amish wedding," my husband replies when I ask him about the possibility. "Every book about Amish life describes Amish wedding customs, often in considerable detail. It's a well-worn subject."

But here I am, already searching for the words to convey what I am seeing and feeling on this early August morning as I hurry with my husband along a gravel road toward the Holmes County, Ohio, farm of the bride's family where an Amish wedding will be held. We have parked the car in the lane of a nearby farm, knowing that most Amish prefer not to have the presence of cars profane their solemn occasions. Ahead and behind us other guests are converging on the site. Dressed in white and black or dark colors, they move steadily across the knolls and dales, past cornfields and pastures toward the barn. Some are in carriages but others walk like us, the neighbors and friends who have come to witness the couple take their vows and commence their life together. At the entrance to the lane someone takes our gift, and I murmur something about not knowing the protocol of an Amish wedding and immediately wish I had said nothing at all. No one around us is talking.

We approach the barn where the bride and groom sit outside on chairs flanked by their four attendants, two men and two women. In English weddings both bride and groom are usually sequestered until the ceremony begins, so we are surprised by their presence and unsure of what to do. Taking our cues from the example of other guests, we shake their hands and express our joy at being invited to their wedding. They express their appreciation for our coming. Then my husband enters the large open area of the barn where the men have already gathered and where the wedding will take place, while I join the women in a smaller room.

The most prominent feature in the room is a large table in the center on which the women's black bonnets have been carefully piled. They are whispering to each other, and one of the younger ones, apparently sensing my feeling of strangeness, offers to sit with me. Promptly at 8:30 the slow, deep tones of the opening hymn serve as a signal for our entrance and we proceed quietly to our benches. Men on one side, women on the other sit facing the center where six chairs conspicuously await the arrival of the bridal party and where the officiating bishop and ministers will soon stand.

Essentially this is an Amish worship service, not much different from a regular Sunday service except that the hymns, scripture, and sermon relate directly to marriage. The Amish family with whom we stayed last night told us what scripture and hymns are traditionally read and sung as well as the subject matter of the officiating bishop's sermon. Among these are readings and admonishments from the apocryphal biblical book Tobit. As the service progresses, I realize that an Amish wedding epitomizes the whole of Amish life: the solemnity, the order, the restraint, the simplicity, the importance of family, community, tradition, and, most especially, the living out of faith.

The congregation begins singing, but it is a while until the bride and groom and their attendants enter quietly and sit on the chairs waiting for them. The bishop and ministers follow soon after and take their places on nearby benches. No grand organ peals out the familiar bridal march, no flowers adorn the front; in fact, there is no front, only a center. Nor is there a self-conscious and lavishly adorned bride. Instead of wearing an elaborate—and expensive—white gown, the bride looks like the other women gathered in her honor except that both she and her attendants wear black organdy prayer caps rather than white ones. (This is the last time the bride will wear the black prayer cap, which is worn only by young, unmarried women.) Dressed in navy blue dresses with white organdy capes and aprons, they sit solemnly on their chairs across from the groom and his attendants, who are clad in plain black suits. Rather than making them distinctive, the clothing of the bride and groom suggests their position as part of the community. It also demonstrates the simplicity and practicality typical of their culture. The Amish wedding ceremony is more than a commitment of the groom and bride to each other: it is a commitment to a way of life.

From where I am sitting I can clearly observe the face of the bride, who appears thoughtful and solemn throughout the morning rituals. After the opening hymns comes the *Anfang*, or short devotional sermon, which lasts the customary half hour. This is followed by the usual prayer and scripture, then the long sermon, preached by the bishop.

Sometimes after joining church, a young Amish person may hedge a bit concerning compliance with the Ordnung, but when he or she marries, dalliance with English temptations usually stops. I recall visiting the house of Amish friends whose daughter was visiting after having been married a few months before. I remembered her as a laughing teenager, full of vitality—even a lighthearted mischief. That day she stood before me as prim as any middle-aged matron, her neat covering hiding her beautiful hair, her cape dress as modest and plain as any Amish husband could desire. Obviously she had assumed the responsibilities that came with her wedding vows as well as the rights and privileges thereof, and while I hoped the lightheartedness remained, it was carefully controlled.

No question exists concerning who is in charge in an Amish household, although often considerable "give and take" occurs in the interactions between a loving couple. A writer in the Amish magazine *Family Life* admonishes women that the wife "was not hired to be the manager or consultant, but she is to be the helpmeet to her husband, to keep the home, to love him, bear children, and to share the responsibility of bringing them up in the fear of the Lord."[1] Articles like this cite the usual passages in the New Testament to support the hierarchical position. Typically these include I Peter 3:4, admonishing women to demonstrate the "ornament of a meek and quiet spirit"; Titus 2:5, commanding women to be "keepers at home, obedient to their husbands"; and Ephesians 5:22, "Wives submit yourselves to your husbands as unto the Lord" (KJV).

On one occasion Amish friends of ours had a disagreement about whether the church service scheduled for their home the following Sunday should be held in the house, which involved a considerable amount of moving of furniture and partitions, or in the barn, which required a considerable amount of cleaning. The husband voted for the house and the wife for the barn. Upon greeting the wife at the entrance to the barn the next Sunday morning, I exclaimed, "Anna, you won!" By the expression on her face, I realized I had said the wrong thing. A wife does not "win"; she may reason and attempt to convince—even cajole and manipulate, perhaps?—but ideally, if not always in practice, she submits to the will of her husband.

---

1. This material and the following letters are taken from "Answers to Maturity in Marriage," *Family Life*, Jan. 1975, 23–29.

In the English world, the traditional roles of men and women, husbands and wives, are being challenged by persons both in and out of the church. The intent of various scriptural passages is being reexamined and reinterpreted, and the debate over these issues has become a dominant concern, at times dividing Christian groups from each other. However, Amish communities have remained aloof from such controversy. Also, for them, divorce is not an option: marriage is for life. Persons in the Amish community who have been divorced by spouses who have left the church are expected to remain unmarried for the remainder of their lives, unless their former spouse dies. Chances are that few—if any—of the women seated around me, married or unmarried, would question these sanctions.

Of course, this does not mean that Amish marriages are perfect. Sometimes spouses just don't "get along," which members of their communities may know—and may even gossip about. More often dissension is covered up: to confess to marital problems is often deemed both shameful and disloyal. Occasionally we hear stories of serious abuse—physical, sexual, and psychological—as well as tales of adulteries and affairs. While these are not common, one Amishman confided that he knows at least ten marriages in which the husband is abusive. And at times situations have been so severe that they have required the intervention of extended family members, church leaders, and even civil authorities, although, in general, the Amish are reluctant to intervene and especially to have outsiders interfere.

It is easy, though, to adopt the tourist mentality and embrace an idealistic hope that the Amish are indeed different from the rest of us, more holy, and less subject to the foibles and sins that plague humankind. However, one young Amishman implied that if divorce were an option, some Amish persons would opt for getting out almost as quickly as some non-Amish couples do. If that is true, then the sociologists who stress the importance of social sanctions in Amish life may be correct—that the strong taboo against divorce is, to a great extent, responsible for the durability of Amish marriage. I'd like to think that he and they are wrong.

Articles and letters on marriage do appear frequently in Amish publications. In one section of *Family Life*, Amish readers typically respond to a "problem" situation presented in the previous issue. In one issue a writer wrote with some disappointment about the happiness of marriage wearing off and declared that the honeymoon never lasted beyond the first year. The column's writer observes realistically: "What percentage of marriages are unhappy among the plain people? That question is hard to answer. Certainly it would not be safe to base any percentage figures on the replies we received in answer to [the inquirer's] statement—out of 74 replies, only one admitted that their marriage is unhappy today. It is likely that most of the people with unhappy marriages simply did not write." A "Mrs. K." from Indiana responds,

> Does the honeymoon last? Maybe not the first "glow" but something far deeper. No, I can't say the first year was the happiest. I would say "now" is the happiest and last year the years before were, too. I'm sure our love is far deeper than when we got married. We have no secret formula. It's in the Bible for all to see. Ephesians 4:32, "And be ye kind one to another, tenderhearted, forgiving one another, even as God for Christ's sake hath forgiven you" is not just for married folks, but is an important ingredient in a happy marriage. I know I get tired and upset sometimes, but we never carry anger into the next day. We also kneel together for prayer each night. If we esteem each other higher than ourselves, we have fewer problems. Of course, I have an unusually good-natured husband and God has greatly blessed us together for over 20 years.

A wife from Ephrata, Pennsylvania, writes:

> The first months of our married life were the hardest for me. I thought I was deeply in love when we got married, but the everyday living was a give-and-take I had not considered. I resented any advice or criticism from my husband. For example, when he advised me on how to cook or do things in the house, I resented his unasked-for suggestions. With the Lord's help, I learned to put humor into these situations. I also learned to discuss differences of opinion maturely. But most important of all, I learned to trust the Lord to help me overlook my husband's shortcomings. Our home is far from perfect, but our love for each other and for the Lord is growing more deeper and more meaningful.

I ponder the sober faces around me. If those letters are a barometer of marital satisfaction, then perhaps we ought to look more closely at what made these married Amish people respond as they did. Are Amish marriages in general more satisfying than English marriages, or are these seventy-three positive responses merely the result of self-selection? What could these people tell me and my culture about marriage that we could profit from, if only they were willing to speak—and if only we were willing to listen? Does a kind of mutual submission exist in the everyday working out of a successful marriage relationship despite a theoretical emphasis on male headship? Or is the hierarchical structure an essential ingredient in their marital equation? Is the emphasis on community—on others rather than on self—a factor in their success? Whatever the answer, most likely we English would be unwilling to accept the terms on which Amish marriage is based.

I suspend my musings when another English couple enter the barn and sit together on a bench behind the youth, and a little later a handful of young men dressed in English clothes slip in and sit near the door. It is 10:30. Surely now it must be time for the minister to stop preaching and for the couple to exchange vows. But not yet. At 10:50 about two dozen young women acting as servers and cooks enter on the women's side, taking the remaining benches or standing along one of the aisles as a group of young men come in on the men's side. Silent and motionless, over four hundred of us now wait for the couple to be officially married. Eleven o'clock comes and goes, and still the admonitions of the bishop continue.

Then, promptly at 11:30, the couple rises and stands before the bishop, the groom first and the bride following. Our host last night informed us that while this may seem discourteous to us English, it is symbolic of the Amish concept of the husband's headship.

The attention of all present is centered on the couple, but they give no evidence of self-consciousness. They do not look at either the bishop or each other. Instead, with averted eyes, they stand solemn and still, concentrating on the bishop's words and responding quietly and deliberately to the vows, which our Amish host later translated for us:

Question: Do you believe and confess that it is the scriptural order for one man and woman to be united and acknowledge that you have begun this relationship in the fear of the Lord?
(Answer: Yes.)
Question: Can you state, brother, that the Lord directs you to take this sister as your wife?

(Answer: Yes.)

Question: Can you state, sister, that the Lord directs you to take this brother as your husband?

(Answer: Yes.)

Question: Do you promise to support your wife when she is in weakness, sickness, and the trials that befall you and stand by her as a Christian husband?

(Answer: Yes.)

Question: Do you promise to support your husband when he is in weakness, sickness, the trails that befall you and stand by him as a Christian wife?

(Answer: Yes.)

Question: Can you vow to remain together and have love, compassion, and patience for one another and not to part from one another until the beloved God shall part you in death?

(Answer: Yes.)

Next follow the prayer and pronouncement, still in German, "So as Raguel took the hand of his daughter and placed it in Tobias's hand and said, 'May the God of Abraham, and the God of Isaac, and the God of Jacob be with you and help and guide you and give His blessings richly to you.' Through Jesus Christ, Amen." At this point the couple genuflects, and with the groom once again leading, they return to their chairs. The wedding ceremony itself has taken less than three minutes, and when the couple is seated, those persons who will serve at the reception quietly file out. After a prayer and a final hymn, the service ends at about 11:50, and I rejoin my husband for the reception that follows.

The reception is held in another building near the house itself, which has been decorated—albeit conservatively—for the occasion. White tablecloths cover the tables, each of which has a small vase of flowers at its center. Beside each place setting is either a royal blue or white napkin with the name of the bride and groom and the date embossed on it. We are given positions across from the table where the bride and groom sit at the corner surrounded by their attendants. This corner, known as the *Eck*, is at one side of the tables rather than at the center. In front of the bride and groom is a three-tiered cake topped with a bouquet of white roses, baby's breath, and ferns. Similar bouquets adorn the table in front of the attendants. Other guests sit on both sides of the wedding party, so rather than having a special table all to themselves, they do indeed have only an Eck. Once again both simplicity and community are present.

The importance placed on this simplicity becomes evident to me later when I discuss wedding traditions with an Old Order Amish acquaintance. She remarks that many Amish weddings are becoming too fancy—too much color is used, too many flowers, and even lace tablecloths instead of plain plastic ones. Why can't people keep things plain and simple, she laments, the way things ought to be? Such fanciness will result in competition and hard feelings, she warns, as it does at a lot of English weddings. Probably she would have disapproved of the accoutrements at this one.

The wedding meal begins with silent prayer. No one introduces the bride and groom or the other members of the wedding party, although other guests tell us that three of the four are siblings of the bride and groom. The bride and her attendants have changed to white prayer coverings, and she and the groom seem relaxed in their corner, greeting with ease the guests who come throughout the meal to wish them well. No one calls out toasts, tells stories about the wedding couple, or clangs silverware against a water glass to lure the bridegroom into kissing the bride, a common custom at many English wedding receptions. Instead, the tone is one of restrained celebration.

The meal is a feast: well-seasoned baked chicken, velvety mashed potatoes, smooth rich gravy, fresh double-cut corn, and a taco salad. This is followed by a jelly roll, ice cream, peach sauce, and two kinds of pie. The servers also pass baskets of candies around the tables in lieu of the traditional favors and offer black coffee to all. The wedding couple does not cut the cake, and I speculate whether that will occur during the meal for the young folk, which will take place at five o' clock in the afternoon. At that time the bride and groom will pair up the young men and women of the community and enjoy a final meal with them before taking on the responsibilities of married life. A silent prayer concludes the meal, after which we mingle with the other guests who enjoy watching the bride and groom open their very practical gifts: towels, sheets, glassware, and even a mailbox. At about 4:30 we say our good-byes, wishing we could stay for the second reception, that of the *Youngie*, or young folk, and observe the pairing off of the couples and the ways in which this meal differs from the earlier one.

Birth, marriage, death . . . these momentous milestones are bounded and hallowed by the customs of the community. Every event has its traditions, although often the participants cannot explain the reasons for them. Nevertheless, everyone knows his or her place.

Occasionally, however, departures from the usual do occur, and when they do they become the subject of stories that remain in the community for decades. Our Amish host last night related a tale about one Amish wedding that took an unexpected turn. An Amish couple meets with the deacon and bishop before their wedding day as well as in the "counsel room" on the morning of the wedding, and each time they are asked, among other things, whether they are certain regarding the leading of the Lord in the taking of the other person as their spouse. At the ceremony they are asked that question for the final time.

At that particular wedding, our host informed us, the groom appeared hesitant, stammered a bit, then—to the astonishment of the congregation—quickly left the building, deserting the bride at the last moment. The bishop was flabbergasted, not knowing what to do with the guests assembled, the meal prepared, and the unexpected defection of the groom. So on an apparent impulse he asked if any man present would like to step forward to take this woman as his wife. To the surprise of all (or most) of those present, one young man did come forward and state that he wished to do so. When the bishop turned to the young woman and asked if she would have him as her husband, she replied, "Yes." Our host explained that the young man and young woman had courted earlier but had broken things off. Supposedly at that time the groom stepped in and eventually proposed marriage, but apparently had experienced second thoughts, so the events weren't as unlikely as they seemed. The wedding went on as planned with the substitute groom.

"Now, Sam," I chided our host, knowing his reputation as a careful researcher of Amish history who would value establishing the truth about such stories, "that sounds incredible to me. Do you really believe it happened?"

"I think so," he responded, somewhat hesitant after I had challenged him. "That story has been around for a long time. I've always assumed it was true. I'll have to check with the others at the next historical meeting."

I waited a couple of years for his reply. Perhaps I should have asked our host what he knows about the "success" of the bride and substitute groom's marriage, but I can guess what probably happened: regardless of the compatibility of the wife and husband, chances are they stayed together till death parted them.

Then, finally, I reminded our historian friend that he had not yet verified the validity of the story. Very soon afterward I received a copy of a German version of the incident with an English translation of the passage, commenting that it took place among the Amish in the Palatinate or Holland around 1780:

> It once occurred, that as the bridegroom stood before the minister [to be married], that his intended bride did not come to him, but left the room. The bridegroom remained standing beside the minister and said unhesitatingly: "If any [lady] has the desire and love thereto, let her come here and stand by my side." Then a young lady was inspired to get up and stand by him. And as they [the bridegroom and the bride] were admonished by the minister and asked the vows, they both answered, "Yes!" And thus they were united in marriage, and lived peacefully and blessedly together. The one who walked outside was punished.[2]

I was astonished at his producing evidence, still questionable, of course, and wondered why the earlier version he told me depicted the deserter as the groom rather than the bride. I also wondered what kind of punishment the unwilling bride received.

Meanwhile, I have conjectured why this story has persisted for over two hundred years in Amish circles. Maybe people repeat this wedding tale simply because it is so uncharacteristic of the Amish way—because it is, in fact, so unlikely. Given the seriousness with which the Amish approach courtship and marriage, I can't imagine a bishop even considering asking if some man would take the place of a renegade bride or groom. Perhaps the story is the Amish equivalent of an urban legend.

But then again . . . maybe the tale persists because it is true.

2. Hans Nafsinger, *Ein Alter Brief* [An Old Letter], trans. Edward Kline, Mar. 26, 1781 (Elkhart, Ind.: Mennonite Publishing House, 1916), 16.

⌁ 6 *⁓*

100 Quilts, 200 Pies, and
Lots of Other Stuff

U sually I travel this four-lane highway on my way to classes at a large urbane and impersonal state university. On this warm August day, however, my husband and I turn off onto a back road and in a few minutes find ourselves in a different world—a smaller one that values piety, simplicity, and community.

We park our car in the field beyond the lines of horses and carriages, mostly black, square-cornered plain carriages, some with open fronts, and one or two of the more rare "white-toppers," buggies with white canvas on their upper sections. Rows of farm implements, old and new furniture, and gadgets of all kinds surround the small, white, clapboard one-room school and the large brown tent and several smaller ones adjoining it. The school is the reason for the gathering.

School sales are common in various Amish settlements, providing half or more of the money necessary to run the Amish parochial schools. These operate on a budget estimated to be approximately 5 percent of the amount expended by comparable public elementary or middle schools. Concentrating on the "three Rs," they do not require the funding for "frills" such as musical instruments, physical education equipment, or computers. Still, teachers must be paid and each small building must be maintained and heated. So members from that area donate various goods for benefit sales—everything from old ringer washing machines and primitive farm equipment to exquisitely detailed quilts and a wide assortment of baked goods. On our way to the main tent we stop to admire a wooden toy chest and a bent wood hickory rocker.

The quilts, which pique my interest most, hang over long ropes in the schoolhouse, each one numbered and labeled according to size and pattern, awaiting the auction time of one o'clock. My husband, of course, is most interested in the people. He is fascinated by the mix of plain and fancy individuals milling around the various tents, creating the impression of a regional fair or even a carnival, which of course this is not.

"That's a Renno Amishman over there," he whispers discreetly. "See, he has only one strap holding up his pants. They're considerably more progressive than the Nebraska Amish," he informs me.

The Nebraskas are one of the most conservative of all the Amish groups. The Nebraska men wear brown pants, no suspenders, and wide-brimmed straw hats with a narrow white band, unlike the Lancaster Amish who wear black pants, suspenders, and black-banded straw hats (at this time of year) or men in some of the Midwestern states who prefer denim pants—with suspenders.

"The Nebraskas ride in plain, white-topped buggies like the one we saw parked back there," my husband continues. "Also, they don't use window screens or plant flowers in their yards."

"Hmm," I respond. "Doesn't God make the brightly colored flowers and birds?"

He laughs. "Ah, come on now. Flowers and birds aren't tempted to pride."

Scanning the crowd, we observe several Nebraska Amishwomen whom we identify by their pleated and wide-brimmed white head coverings and their pointed cape dresses. They seem to favor various shades of blue and purple, often wearing aprons that are a different shade from their dresses. I also note some plain Mennonite women distinguishable by their small-print dresses and some Amish Mennonite little girls with their long braids and no head coverings. These plain people mingle together with English people wearing shorts, sandals or athletic shoes with name-brand labels, and T-shirts resembling billboards.

We enter a tent where a variety of food is for sale: subs, hot dogs, barbecue sandwiches, chicken corn and ham and bean soups, and fresh fruit salad. I choose a cup of chicken corn soup and a summer fruit cup. My husband orders a pork barbeque sandwich and a glass of iced spearmint tea, an Amish favorite known locally as "meadow tea." Just outside the tent we note the school water pump where some barefooted Amish boys, who were sent to get water for lemonade, are spraying each other instead. Beyond them along the fence is a row of wooden pie safes, each capable of holding a dozen or so pies or coffee cakes or loaves of homemade bread. That reminds me that we haven't yet picked out our dessert.

We approach the pie table, which offers as large a selection of pies as a Burpee seed catalog does tomatoes: apple and a dried apple variety known as Schnitz, blueberry, blackberry, cherry, raisin, and—of course—shoofly pie. My husband settles for a piece of blackberry, and

I happily locate a piece of lemon sponge, hoping that it is as good as that made from a recipe passed down in my family. I remember that the recipe states, "Cream butter the size of a walnut." I never have been able to figure out whether that means a shelled or unshelled nut.

We find places at a bench and table and listen to the rhythmic patter of the auctioneer in the quilt tent nearby. I am eager to finish eating and to see as many of the quilts as I can, but—of course—my husband wants to talk. Across the way he spies an Amishman he knows and hurries off to chat with him, leaving me with strangers. Soon he motions me to join him.

He introduces me to an Amish minister at whose house he has stayed, and I greet him as pleasantly as I can. I am ill at ease in situations like this, knowing that whenever someone has met my husband without seeing me and has accepted him as a friend, most likely that person assumes that I am a plain Mennonite who wears a prayer "cap," if not a covering, and a cape dress. Here I stand in a white blouse and denim skirt—which ought to be acceptable—but with short hair. Probably he is wondering why a woman old enough to be a grandmother and the wife of a man who wears a beard would cut her hair.

I watch him steal a look at my head and then at my husband, who is chattering away, oblivious to it all. Of course, the man is not going to ask me why I cut my hair, nor will I inquire what is so sacred about wearing black. But experiencing his jovial laugh and firm handshake, I have a hunch that we will become friends. Despite our differences we are both people of faith, specifically of Anabaptist persuasion.

Next we meet two of his daughters, one of whom we have previously greeted at the pie table without knowing her identity, and the other who is working at the hot dog stand. Already young wives and mothers, they demonstrate the quiet poise and lack of affectation of Amishwomen who are both competent and at ease in their world.

Nothing in their demeanor clamors for attention. They are attired in the typical plain dresses fastened with straight pins and wear the larger, more distinctly shaped, opaque white prayer coverings with detailed pleating, rather than the semitransparent, softer, almost heart-shaped ones I see in Lancaster County. Looking at their clear, unadorned faces, I decide that their plainness only enhances their beauty.

But I am most eager to see the quilts. More than a hundred of them are being auctioned off, and I don't want to miss seeing any more of them than I already have. However, our friend points out an Amishman on the other side of the tent who lives in the same county in another state where we once lived. So we trudge off in his direction, making our way around Amish parents holding the hands of awed children and English visitors clutching purses and wallets whose contents will help to refill the coffers of this Amish school.

After brief introductions, we begin the "who-do-you-know-that-I-know" game since obviously, not being Amish, we can't play the "who-are-you-related-to-that-I-am-related-to" one. In contrast to mainstream American custom, when Amish people are introduced to one another, they rarely ask, "What do you do?" meaning "What is your position in life?"—or more specifically, "How far up the status ladder are you?" Eventually someone will be identified as a farmer or a carpenter or the like, and upon inquiry my husband will say that he teaches at a college, specifically on the subject of youth, but he rarely identifies himself as a professor of psychology.

And they assume that I am just a housewife—which has value in their community but little status in ours. On first acquaintance I don't usually reveal that I also teach on the college level as an adjunct instructor, especially since my field of literature is difficult to justify in their society. Sometimes I do admit that I teach writing, which is more acceptable because it can be considered a practical skill. A friend of ours, who has done considerable research on some Amish customs and has published a book on her findings, reports that all of her degrees and accomplishments count for little in the Amish community.

At last we get to the tent where they are auctioning off the quilts. We locate seats by an English couple who are serious shoppers, assiduously perusing the quilt guide booklet they have bought, having already decided on some possible purchases. Several men hold up each quilt in front of the assemblage as the auctioneer identifies and describes it, almost always remarking, "Now that's a purty one." He then commences his chanting at what he considers to be the lowest acceptable bid.

Quickly the bidders respond, clutching their placards on which their preassigned numbers are printed. A raised finger or a nod pushes the bid up a notch. The auctioneer looks at the previous bidder or at another bidder across the aisle who has shown interest while carrying on his singsong chant. Excitement rises as more and more bidders drop out and only the serious two or three remain. Finally the auctioneer pounds his gavel and cries, "Sold!" I alternately lean forward and then sit back, deliciously enjoying the artistry of the quilts displayed, the drama of each sale, and the staccato rise and fall of the auctioneer's voice.

The patterns are well-known: log cabin and its variations, turkey track, Dresden plate, Irish chain, trip around the world, the various star designs, and even a few double-wedding rings. Some are softly colored, others are crafted of more vivid shades, but they usually combine both plain and patterned fabrics, having been created specifically for this sale. Few truly "Amish" quilts are offered for sale—the geometric patterned, brightly colored ones that juxtapose purple, blue, green, and a lot of black. The quilts bring varying amounts, $300, $500, $800, depending on size, quality, and general appeal. I note that they sell for much less, however, than they would in settlements where more tourists visit.

The excitement grows again when the auctioneer realizes that two different bidders are bent on getting one particular quilt. The crowd watches breathlessly as the bidding reaches "nine and one-half" ($950) and the other bidder hesitates to push the bid higher.

"She really wants it, Larry," the auctioneer prods the man who has been bidding for the woman beside him. The bid goes to $975, and again there is a pause.

"I'd like to get a thousand dollars out of this quilt," the auctioneer declares, and suddenly it is done. The crowd breaks into applause, chattering their satisfaction to one another, and then another quilt is brought out for display and the bidding starts anew.

And so it goes until the last quilt is sold and the crowd disperses, some people to their cars and buggies, some to peruse the wares in the schoolhouse, and some to the field beyond where another auctioneer already has begun selling vintage farm equipment and other such gadgets, many of them relics from an earlier era. We work our way through the crowd back to the car, and soon are headed down the four-lane highway toward home.

The activities at the school and the mixture of Amish groups remind me once again of the paradoxes of Amish community with its strengths and its weaknesses. Sales such as this one are held frequently. They demonstrate how Amish communities work together toward a common goal, in this case, raising the necessary funds for the education of the children of the local area. Sometimes sales are held to aid a family experiencing a financial crisis because of the hospitalization of a child or other family member. Since the Amish do not believe in any kind of commercial insurance, the catastrophic bills that result from any extended health care are beyond the ability of the average Amish family to pay. Church and friends provide significant aid in times of disaster.

The most visible—and famous—assistance of this kind is, of course, an Amish barn raising. When a series of tornadoes leveled more than a half dozen barns one spring in Somerset County, Pennsylvania, the local Amish community organized a succession of barn raisings in the next few weeks that drew busloads of Amish from other counties and states. Their concerted efforts over a period of several weeks resulted in the rebuilding of not only several of the barns of their members, but also some of those of their English neighbors, including those who had cursed God and had at first stubbornly resisted outside help.

But if the cohesiveness of Amish community is evident at barn raisings and school sales, so also are the markings of their divisiveness. When someone asks, "Don't all Amish . . . ?" I find myself hesitating and then replying, "Yes, but. . . ." Always within the settlement lurks the issue of how much technology should be permitted—or from the vantage point of some members, how much change of any kind should be tolerated. The watchword in general is *so hem miss Noah immer geduh*—"so we have always done it." One Amish bishop confessed, "Some of our people make a religion out of not changing."

The use of technology varies considerably from group to group. Some settlements allow tractors—rather than the typical horses or mules—with the stipulation that the tires must be metal rather than rubber. Regulations regarding telephone usage vary greatly according to settlement: members of New Order Amish use them as freely as members of mainstream society; one Old Order settlement dictates that they may be used for outgoing but not incoming calls; and the Nebraska settlements are supposed to use them only for emergencies. Cell phones are relatively common in many communities.

In some cases technological adjustments become necessary just for economic survival, as when bulk milk tanks and milking machines were introduced in Lancaster County, Pennsylvania, in response to state laws regulating the practices of farmers who wanted their milk marketed as Grade A quality. In Holmes County, Ohio, the response to similar legislation resulted in some groups settling for Grade B milk and the eventual establishment of local cheese factories, now so popular with tourists.

While the drift generally is toward a very controlled and gradual modernization, a few groups have, in Amish parlance, deliberately chosen to "drift backward," opting for no motorized equipment of any kind. They eschew refrigerators, employ only animals in farmwork, and resort to hand water pumps in the kitchens. One reactionary group resisted the use of numbers on mailboxes, wanting nothing that would tie them into mainstream society. Another decided that men could no longer wear the "clip" style of suspenders, but must wear the "buttonhole" kind. Supposedly, one of the most conservative groups won't allow their men to wear elastic in their long johns and has determined that T-shirts must be altered to have plackets in their fronts.

Differences extend to worship practices as well. For example, everyone "knows" that Old Order Amish church services are conducted in houses, barns, or shops. Not so: a group of districts in Somerset County, Pennsylvania, meet in buildings which they designate as meetinghouses, not churches, since according to their beliefs, the church is the community of people who meet to worship rather than the building where they assemble. And while most Amish worship services are restrained, those in a couple of maverick settlements have become charismatic, adopting some patterns more typical of the Pentecostals.

Usually regulations are the result of genuine religious conviction. But at times the church splits that appear to outsiders to stem from legalism. In some cases, Amish individuals have confided that underneath the apparent divisions over technology and dress lie personality or power conflicts.

Tourists who drive through Holmes County and admire the togetherness of the Amish community might be surprised to find out that many of the Amish persons who greet each other at the auction or the supermarket cannot take communion with one another at the semiannual communion services. Who may and who may not "commune" (fellowship) with another Amish group is determined by the congregations of the respective districts, and only those groups with similar Ordnungs will permit this kind of interaction.

Plain clothes, strict standards of conduct, and common traditions cannot bring about true community. Dissension cannot be barricaded out by rules and rituals. Like the worm in the apple, it lurks within, waiting to spoil and destroy, whether the society is Amish or English.

. 7 *~*

Amos Speaks His Mind

H is wife greets us at the door of their house and introduces him to my husband and me. I like him immediately; later I realize this is partly because he resembles my husband. Almost the same age, they demonstrate the same ease with people—the ability to inspire them to open up and communicate on deeper levels rather than merely engaging in perfunctory small talk. It is a case of friendship at first sight.

Soon he is sharing his love of history and of reading as well as his frustrations with parenting and his concerns for the church district of which he is a member. Quickly I ascertain that he is wise in the ways of the business world, aware of the foibles of human nature, and sensitive to the complexities of human relationships and human institutions. An astute businessman, he criticizes the managers of the market where he works for their lack of business savvy: the dirty stands, the inadequate parking, the dearth of general marketing strategies.

He is, I discover later, fascinated with motors, including automobile engines, and offers to help my husband locate a problem with one of our cars, one that no professional mechanic has been able to correct. If man can make it, he insists, man can fix it. Later the blend of his attraction to both people and machines come together on a trip when we stop for lunch at a roadside picnic area. He strikes up a conversation with a motorcyclist, which leads eventually to a demonstration of his expensive machine—but not a ride.

Although he may be attracted to certain aspects of English life, he is not a "fence-sitter." Like many Amish, he has deliberately chosen to embrace the tradition in which he was reared. But his openness to the world beyond—and his nontraditional ways of viewing his own community—sets him apart from the norm. He has English friends in Maine and Kentucky whom he and his wife visit. On Sundays when he cannot attend his own district services, he attends the local Baptist services, including the Sunday school class. He has a working relationship with his Latino neighbors and values their culture, unlike some of his other neighbors who think their ways strange. On the way to Sunday service he points out a bird-carving shop, a cemetery in which a famous person is buried, and a cobblestone house.

He explains the customs and behaviors of his settlement and interprets their meanings for us. He points out that in his own Amish services, not all the men who have their eyes closed during the morning service are sleeping; rather, he says, because there has been some talk of men looking too long at the women, they have learned to avoid suspicion by bowing their heads.

But he goes beyond mere interpretations of Amish customs; he evaluates them as well, showing a willingness to alter traditions that do not truly fit in with the spirit of Amish culture. The really important things, he insists, are love and unity within the community. His critiques purport to be from the viewpoint of an insider who wants to purify and refine. Well, mostly. Sometimes I suspect that he really wants to find ways to do some things that are not allowed.

He tells us that unless a particular practice is expressly forbidden, it can be assumed to be permitted. In addition, he observes that while some things may be "frowned upon," they are not a "test of membership." And, he points out, some things that could be objectionable will be tolerated if they are performed discreetly. He cites the example of an older man who has a wood shop in his basement, running the power equipment off his diesel. Since few people know, no one objects, and no contention develops. Is this the reasoning behind the presence of computers, fax machines, cell phones, hair dryers, and whirlpools that run on inverters (which change one kind of electrical energy to another) in the back rooms of some Amish homes, I wonder? Is Amos's rationalization for his own subtle violations of the Ordnung, such as running an extension cord from the neighbor's shed to power a fan—which we discover when we stop by later when no one is at home—widespread in Amish settlements?

"What do you think the future of the Amish community is?" he asks.

I am not going to be baited by that question. Neither is my husband. We turn it back to him.

He can hardly wait to tell us.

Sometime in the near future, he postulates, his own district will split over the automobile. Already some of the young people are asking why they can ride to work in cars and vans every day except Sunday, but not own them. Thirty years ago when he was young, about 90 percent of the young people in his settlement went into farming and the rest into other occupations, mostly carpentry. Now it is just the opposite. Now only 10 percent go into farming and 90 percent work in jobs that are too far away from home for them to use a horse and buggy for transportation. So they are forced to hire non-Amish men to drive them to and from work in vans.

And that has created special problems, he declares. Because the van drivers tend to be "fringy" and to have low morals, he asserts, this places the most vulnerable members of the Amish community, teenaged males, in situations of temptation that they would not face if they were allowed to own vehicles and drive them only to and from work, not even stopping at the store on the way home for a loaf of bread. They could continue to use their traditional horses and carriages for all other occasions, he explains.

It is not the vehicle itself that is wrong, he insists, but the way it is used. He knows that many of his fellow Amishmen would disagree and that he is not looked upon favorably because of his views.

Another point of contention regarding the automobile is that some parents allow their wayward sons to park their vehicles in plain sight in front of their houses. But what's a person to do—put his own flesh and blood out on the doorstep, thus almost assuring their association with non-Amish young people, and often those of the worst kind? He knows that some youth in his district have been involved with drugs as a result of their association with some English.

Wistfully he remarks that members of the plainest Amish affiliations, such as the Swartzentruber group, are the happiest. Their young people are not allowed to interact with non-Amish any more than is absolutely necessary, thus avoiding many of the temptations which the children of more liberal Amish face. I nod with understanding. In many ways it is easier and more comfortable to live in isolation from the complexities and ambiguities of human existence, but I do not say this aloud.

He does not envy the bishops and ministers the challenges they have in dealing with such issues as these, he declares. He would not want to be in their shoes. He thinks he is old enough not to have to worry about being nominated and having his name placed on the list from which the name of the minister-to-be will be chosen by lot.

Don't be so sure about that, his wife cautions, citing a minister who was older than he is when chosen.

Whereupon he launches into a detailed explanation of the way ministers are chosen in their area. Each Amish church member nominates one man, and the names of those who have at least three votes are included in the drawing by lot. At either the spring or the fall communion service, the nominees take turns choosing a book from among those which have been prepared for this purpose. The man who chooses the book containing a piece of paper is the new minister and is ordained on the spot.

Our host confides that he has observed some men acting as though they are campaigning for office as the time for the choosing of a minister draws near. However, those men, he observes, are not likely to receive the votes of their fellow church members. After all, most people aren't that stupid.

We mention several of our Amish friends who have become ministers or bishops since we have known them. They have told us about the fearful sense of responsibility they felt upon their ordination. My husband recalls one Amishman who jokingly declared that if he thought people were considering voting for his nomination, he would ride around the community in a motorcycle just to make sure they wouldn't submit his name.

He nods his head and clutches his beard. He wouldn't want the responsibility of all those souls, he asserts. But, of course, there are less obvious ways of deflecting votes. One can always cut one's hair a bit shorter than is the custom and shape it to the head. That is enough to put some people off.

We inquire about how he feels concerning the latest ruling by the settlement bishops declaring that no Amish person may take part in softball games, until recently a widely enjoyed activity. And not only is participation forbidden, but also attendance as spectators, and the washing of softball uniforms. Only under the supervision of an Amish teacher at an Amish school is softball to be allowed.

He shakes his head in disbelief. A bad move on their part, he asserts—a very bad move. It will do just the opposite of what the bishops intend. It's going to keep a lot of young people from joining church, and the delay will cause them to get involved in other, more dangerous activities. We nod noncommittally and change the subject.

We talk over pie and coffee, planning a future visit—maybe a hike or a trip to a nearby historical site. We are relaxed in each other's presence. When I confess that I struggle with insomnia, he confidently asserts that overcoming this is a matter of attitude: You just have to clear your mind of the things that are bothering you and decide to sleep. It's as simple as that.

I have barely met them, but I feel as though I have known them for a long time and that we have a lot in common. As we say good bye at their door, I look more closely at the style of his hair. It is definitely shorter than that of the average Amishman his age and very attractively shaped to his head.

❧ 8 ❧

A Patchwork of Amish Women

Seven or eight "plain" women have gathered around a quilting frame in the otherwise empty garage of a Florida winter cottage, the untied white strings of their prayer coverings dangling onto their shoulders. The large quilt they are working on is a variation of the "log cabin" pattern known as "log cabin star." Hunter green and cranberry patterns stand out against its white background, although the patchwork includes calicoes of various prints in complementary colors. The sharp corners of the pieces and the smoothness of the seams testify to the precise workmanship of its maker, a sprightly woman in her eighties.

With one hand under the quilt and the other on top deftly manipulating needle, thumb, thimble, and finger back and forth in a rhythmic motion, the women make fast progress, producing tiny stitches and creating wondrous geometric designs that outline and accent the pieces in the pattern. Together they can accomplish in three or four days what would take one woman quilting alone weeks or months to finish. Photographers who like to portray images of Amish community frequently feature either a scene like this or its masculine counterpart: an Amish barn raising. Such activities have become metaphors for Amish life.

Although I can identify the approximate geographical area the women have come from by the shape, size, and stiffness of the fabric of their prayer coverings, I recognize how much more similar the details of their clothing are than they are different. Old Order Amishwomen wear plain-cut dresses fitted loosely at the waist and sometimes fashioned with a capelike appendage over the bodice. Straight pins rather than buttons close the dresses in front, reputedly because buttons connote the military, which, of course, the Amish, who oppose war, do not want to imitate.

Most older Old Order Amishwomen choose subdued colors, such as blue, brown, maroon, or gray, but brighter and lighter shades are common among the younger ones. Black predominates among the older women because black is worn for varying periods after the death of a relative, depending on the closeness of the relative who has died, and older women are more likely to have experienced the deaths of near relatives than younger ones. Favored colors among younger women include vary-ing shades of blue and even purple. Red, however, is forbidden, and only in the more liberal settlements will the women wear yellow or pink. Old Order women also shun prints and trim of any kind, and any evidence of these suggests slippage and a possible move toward liberalization. While sleeve length varies from settlement to settlement, the trend is toward longer ones, and skirts extend below their calves; in the most conserva-tive settlements, skirts almost touch the shoes.

On church Sundays when the older women assemble in the kitchen or yard prior to the morning service, they look like the little Amish dolls perched on a shelf in some tourist-catching gift shop. Dressed in their black capes, black shoes, dark dresses, and pleated black bonnets, they resemble each other so closely that one is tempted to assume they *are* alike. And, of course, to some extent this is true, since all members of a church district must abide by the Ordnung of that district, which be-comes the pattern onto which they stitch their lives.

What I have discovered, however, is that the ways in which they fol-low that pattern are as kaleidoscopic as the quilts they craft.

Emma likes to cook. With a husband and seven children, she has good reason to cook often and the motivation to cook well. Her kitchen is much plainer than those I have visited in Lancaster County and contains more primitive equipment. She uses a wood stove, telling us that yes, it took a while to learn how to gauge the heat, but that now she prefers it to the gas stoves she used while growing up. Her kitchen has no run-ning water, only two sinks with drains, one for washing food and dishes and the other for washing hands. A water pump is in an adjoining room down a short flight of stairs. She keeps the food cold in an icebox located in a large walk-in closet inside the pump room, which means that she must purchase a twenty-five-pound block of ice every week in the sum-mer. If that melts before the iceman returns, someone drives over in the buggy to a local store and purchases additional ice, she tells me.

On the day of our visit—a warm day in July—her kitchen is a verita-ble bakery; the large table is brimming with plump loaves of bread, two kinds of cookies, fruit and meringue pies, rolls, and frosted tea rings, most of which she has prepared for the school sale on the following day. Despite this busyness, she invites us to supper, the warmth of her words assuring us of her genuineness. We accept.

She prepares one of the most delicious meals I have ever eaten—Amish or otherwise. Both she and her two daughters bustle barefoot around the pump room, which apparently serves as a summer kitchen, putting the finishing touches on the meal consisting of oven-fried chicken and lettuce, carrot, and cheese salad, noodles, Jell-O, cherries, several kinds of homemade rolls, home-canned apple juice, and two kinds of pie for dessert. We learn that she has gleaned some of the recipes for the meal from magazines she has read.

Later we gather by lamplight on the large front porch, sitting on chairs, steps, railing, swing, and glider. We eat and talk, enjoying the cool, clear evening. Always, it seems, there is enough time in Amish society to get to know each other better, and, of course, there is no television to compete with human communication. The parents reminisce about their early days on the property when they lived in the basement before they could build the spacious two stories they now enjoy. We watch the purple martins alight on the perches in front of their hollowed-out gourd birdhouses. I admire the begonias lining the porch, flowers I usually manage to kill in my house or garden, but Emma laughs and modestly declares that hers must be so beautiful because the location suits them.

By English standards Emma is deprived and overworked. Apparently no one has told her that, so she exudes an enviable contentment in caring for her home and family and in helping in her husband's shop.

Ada and I are discussing having babies, especially the more difficult of her twelve pregnancies and deliveries. As she talks, she pushes the propane iron across her daughter's white Sunday apron, deftly smoothing out the wrinkles. Her oldest was born in the hospital, she informs me, but the rest were born in a birthing clinic nearby, except for her seven-year-old. Things didn't seem quite right to the doctor, she explains, so he arranged for the baby to be born in a hospital. Possibly a cesarean, they thought, but that wasn't necessary. They were afraid that the cord might get caught around the neck, but it didn't.

Ada has gone through a dozen deliveries, so my three seem paltry by comparison. Two of her children are slightly over a year apart. She accepts her large family as normal, considering children a blessing from the Lord, and her well-run household demonstrates the capacity of many Amishwomen for careful organization and hard work.

Ada confides that she has had her tubes tied—for health reasons which she does not explain. Since the Amish are not supposed to practice birth control, I wonder if *any* plausible "health reason" suffices after a woman has delivered a certain number of children. Another woman I know recently had her tubes tied "for health reasons" after the birth of her seventh son. She didn't seem shy about talking about it, either.

When one of my husband's students mentioned the matter of birth control to a married Amishman, he was informed that the church forbids it. The student was bold enough to ask about abstinence as a possible method of birth control, and the husband responded that it "would take the fun out of life."

᠁

I am walking around the "loop" with Rebecca and two of her three married daughters, Sally and Rachel. The "loop" is a series of country roads that form a circle which will bring us back to the yard where the men are relaxing after a picnic supper in the late afternoon of a "home Sunday"—the alternate Sunday on which no church service is held in this district. Typically, these Sundays are used for attending a service in a neighboring district, resting or visiting friends and relatives.

Our ostensible purpose is to get exercise. A daughter of each of the young women has come along. They walk and skip ahead of us, chatting with the camaraderie typical of cousins who share the same genes and the same experiences. I am surprised to discover that both of these young mothers consider exercise an important part of their daily regimen, as does the grandmother. Rebecca tells me that she sometimes walks before six in the morning. I ask whether she is afraid in the darkness, and she answers no.

Since I am the oldest of the walkers, my Amish companions express concern about my ability to complete the entire route, about two miles, in the shoes that I am wearing, which are low pumps. I assure them that I will be all right: my shoes are comfortable even though they are not my usual walking shoes.

Sally looks ahead at the two young cousins, girls on the verge of puberty. "Don't you envy their tight little buns?" she asks wistfully.

I am astounded both at her choice of words and her concern with their figures. I didn't know Amishwomen cared about such things. And when I told one Amish friend about this incident, her response was, "This type of comment is unheard of. I don't want your reading audience to think it is typical." Whether that friend is correct or not, I cannot say.

Since the news of the death of Princess Diana has recently shocked the world, the conversation during the walk turns to the events surrounding her tragic accident. The women demonstrate their knowledge about the escapades of the royal family and express sadness over the princess's death. They do not admire her lifestyle.

How much of the media do they come into contact with, I wonder. The newspaper, perhaps? Magazines? Perhaps they are not so isolated from mainstream American culture as I previously thought. Have they been exposed to media enough to have absorbed the American obsession with thinness? Or are they genuinely concerned about health? I wonder about these questions as we head back to the house.

⋏ ⋎

"Ours is a marriage not made in heaven," Naomi confesses to my husband laughingly. He can't believe his ears. It's not that he is surprised to find that some Amish couples experience difficulties in relating to each other just as many non-Amish couples do—he already knows some do. But few confess that out loud. Frustrations and disappointments are to be accepted as a part of life, and they certainly should not be aired in public.

Naomi is the "scribe" (letter writer) for her settlement for *Die Botschaft*, one of the Amish newspapers that report the activities of widespread Amish communities. Her letters violate the cultural norms in that rather than merely offering the usual information concerning weather, crops, weddings, guest ministers, births, deaths, illnesses, and social visits, Naomi writes about how she *feels*. Also, she ventures her opinions on matters that might not quite fit the approved patterns. And occasionally she demonstrates unusual transparency by including references to family squabbles.

In an informal survey of Amish *Botschaft* readers, my husband has noted that they either very much like or very much dislike Naomi's writing; few readers are neutral. He has also observed, however, that even those who claim to respond negatively to her letters still admit to reading them regularly.

"I don't like the way she downs her husband," one reader complains when asked about her articles.

"Yeah," his companion responds. "And she's always writing about being too fat. I always assumed she was a big woman, but from what I hear, she isn't."

The other nods. "She's always writing about how she rides the scooter to the store. She scoots here and she scoots there. Why doesn't she just say she went somewhere instead of saying she's scooting around?"

Curious, I collect a group of *Botschafts* and peruse her letters, finding that I enjoy both their candor and their vividness.[1] She describes one minor family disagreement about whether they should stay for the Sunday evening singing this way:

We stayed for supper, and after supper [my husband] was ready to leave. I wanted to stay for the singing, as we haven't attended any since [our daughter] is with the youth. Well, he wasn't going to stay. So I said, "Fine, I'll stay, and go home with [neighbors]." Gulp. Time for a little women's rights here, I thought self-righteously. It was time to take Dad home, so [a friend] took Charlie, our horse, and [my husband] settled in with another cup of coffee and stayed for the singing, too! That was a rare treat, and I was still singing those beautiful songs at the washing machine on Mon. morn. I gave [my husband] a big smile and profusely thanked him for staying.

Her sensitivity and kindly spirit come through in the following excerpt:

Our young people need our trust, and I know it isn't always easy, but somehow, as mysterious as it seems, they desperately need love, trust and only to be accepted. Let us pray for answers and for help along the way. We all want to go to Heaven together, and the "wild ones" do, too.

Concerning her experience hostessing a large group of out-of-town guests as well as many family members for supper, she admits:

Now that was a major nail-biting affair. I am only a so-so cook and no baker at all. The [visiting] people all have a talent with food. They all said it was good, but they were all very polite and kind. The next day when Mom served her food, I thought "Woe is me!"

1. These letters were published in *Die Botschaft*.

How many people, English or Amish, are willing to be that open about their feelings on such a sensitive subject? Probably it is this honesty that appeals to many of her readers. In the same column she continues:

> The peacock remains on the loose, and starts hollering at 4:00 every morn. I always start slamming doors and windows, so I can go back to sleep. I will not write the discussions about the peacock. I would be ashamed. I'm seriously thinking of risking life and limb, climbing the oak tree where he roosts and maybe catching him with a net. Surely I could give him enough Tylenol till I get him to the auction. An overdose sounds just fine to me.

In the final installment on the peacock she rejoices:

> The peacocks are gone! My life is definitely brighter. . . . [My husband] was saying that he'll dig a pond, plant some willow trees and build a little house for us someday when we retire, meaning here in our field. [My son] is still a little perturbed at having to sell his noisy friend, the peacock, so he said, "Yep, then I'll live in this house, and have piles of peacocks. They'll all be hollering at once, and you'll think back to the peaceful days when you heard only one."

However, when the scribe becomes pregnant, my husband inquires of a relative whether that news will go into the *Botschaft*. The quick reply is, "It better not." The violation of social norms may be tolerated to some extent, but there are limits.

My English friends first met Katie when she appeared at their door inquiring if they needed someone to clean their house. Her own house, they tell me, is very tastefully decorated, and only the absence of electricity signals that it is Amish. She is, they tell me, "a real go-getter." She runs a stand at the farmers' market in a nearby city. That means she must get up at four o'clock in the morning on market days in order to transport her wares to market and arrange them.

In addition, she has published a cookbook that has sold more than 300,000 copies. Shrewd businesswoman that she is, she bargained with the printer to defer payment for each of the printings of 50,000 copies until the receipts for the books started to come in from local shops. She is an example of numerous Amishwomen who add to the family income. Most often, their labor allows them to stay at home, perhaps quilting, making crafts, or managing a produce stand at the end of their farm lane, although they also may clean the houses of their English neighbors or sell produce at a local market. But increasingly Amishwomen are managing businesses such as the popular quilt shops located in the larger tourist centers. Some of these establishments handle a large volume of business and their operators deal with people from around the world. These "briefcase carrying" Amish career women must juggle home and church and business while staying within the confines of their rigidly prescribed roles.

I wonder if many men at heart would like an Amish wife—at least at times in their lives—not necessarily the plainness, but the submission and the attention. The hierarchal pattern has its advantages; it is harder to be partners, to negotiate and compromise. On the surface it appears to be easier to have one person in charge who makes the final decisions. However, more and more Englishwomen are finding that pattern stultifying. Do some Amishwomen struggle with it as well?

Arie's dress is not really plain; the dark-blue double knit contains a tiny print. Also, Arie is wearing white canvas tennis shoes and bobby socks over her panty hose. She sports an inconspicuous gold pin on her shoulder, but actually it *is* conspicuous since Amish adults never wear jewelry, not even wedding rings. Rather than pulling her hair back from her face in the severe, twisted style of her settlement—which often results in the loss of hair near the centered part-line in many women—she has arranged hers in a looser, fluffier, more flattering style. And her covering rests further back on her head than is permitted by the local Ordnung, giving her a jaunty appearance.

She sings Sunday school songs along with the college students in the van as we travel together to visit an Amish settlement in another state. She confesses that yes, she has a boyfriend. Although she has joined church, she is dating a young man from an Amish family in his mid-twenties who has not yet joined. He owns a pickup truck—in violation of Amish rules. We know that her parents have two children who have already left the faith, and they worry that Arie will leave also, especially since she is so attached to her young man.

Arie admits that she and a group of her Amish girlfriends have taken trips to the shore in the summer. There they let their hair down, wear shorts, play tennis, and lie on the beach. She also watches television with her friends at the house where she cleans regularly for an English-woman.

Thinking we recognize many danger signs concerning her commitment to the Amish way of life, my husband and I speculate whether or not she will leave the fold.

Several years later we and some friends visit her home, which is as plain and simple as any in the community. She and her husband are the parents of three small children, and gossip has it that one of her older siblings may come back to the fold after all. Her household is run like that of any good Amish wife in the community, and all of her "worldly ways" have been discarded like the cast-off dolls of her childhood.

But we realize just how much she had changed when we ask her if she has copies of a popular book about the Amish that contains pictures taken of her before she "joined church." She replies, "Yes," but we sense her reluctance to show them, so we do not press her.

I remember standing in the doorway of her parents' house when one of those pictures was taken. Dressed in their Sunday clothes and seated in a carriage, she and her sister drove past the house as an author/photographer called at them to look at him. Lifting her chin and turning her head in his direction, she smiled slightly as he snapped the camera.

Years later we ask a young Amishwoman what aspects of the Ordnung are most difficult for young people to follow. She confides that cameras and picture taking are among the last things for Amishwomen to give up because they like to have pictures of their husbands and children.

Arie has given evidence of her commitment to the Amish way of life.

⋈ ⋈

Barbara is wearing knee-length shorts, a white knit top, bright red fingernail polish, and a wedding ring. Her short brown hair is stylishly cut. She takes our order for lunch with an air of confidence and a sense of humor.

Obviously she is not Amish. Yet my husband follows his hunch and queries her.

"Kanst du Dietsch swetsa?" (Do you speak Pennsylvania Dutch?)

"Yah," she responds. Gently he plies her with a few more questions, and before long she is telling us her story.

"Yes, I was Amish," she admits. She names the small settlement where she grew up, which my husband recognizes by name only. It is a relatively new settlement, consisting of only three church districts, she tells us. My husband inquires whether the youth of the settlement look to the adults or to each other for their standards of behavior.

"Lots of problems there," she informs us, shaking her head.

"Why do you think that is so?" my husband asks.

"Power struggles," she responds quickly. "They've been going on for a long time, and I think they'll continue for many more years. Too much fighting for control. It's bad."

"How old were you when you left?" My husband wants to know.

"Twenty-two," she replies, "but I thought about it for about seven years before I did it."

"Seven years!" My husband repeats in amazement. "That's a long time."

She nods. "I didn't know how to break out. I wanted to do it with the least hurt possible for my family. I had to work up the courage."

We understand. We know that Amish parents may feel disappointed, betrayed, or disgraced when their children desert the faith. They also feel like failures. And if the young people have joined church, they will be shunned, depriving them of the support system which has been such an important part of their lives.

"Do you go home very often?"

She shrugs her shoulders. "Not very much anymore. My family was very hurt by my decision to leave. I really respect my father. I did then, and I do now. It was really hard on him at first. When we did talk after I left, we argued about religion. I think the Amish in that church district are mostly following tradition. I don't see much spiritual life there, and when I told my father that he ought to leave himself—he has a real gift for evangelism—he said that he considered it his duty to stay with the church. So we sort of agreed not to talk about things like that. But at least my parents haven't been so hard on my younger brother, who has also left."

"What's it like being ex-Amish?"

"Oh, it's such a big world out here," she motions with a sweep of her hands. "So many options. So much to learn to and to do. I'm taking classes at the university—mostly general education requirements because I'm interested in everything and can't decide on a major."

"So you're finding life outside the Amish community a challenge?" my husband asks.

"Oh, yes!" she exclaims. "So many decisions. When I was Amish, there weren't any decisions to make except for whether or not to stay Amish. After that, almost everything is decided for you, and you just have to live accordingly, whether you like it or not. But at first I felt naive and unprepared for the outside world."

Without knowing it she is confirming a theory my husband has regarding why it would be so difficult for "Englishers" to become Amish. He believes that it would not be the giving up of the modern conveniences such as cars or telephones or electricity that would be so difficult, rather it would be the loss of individual choice.

Barbara appears to be enjoying her newfound freedom. But we also know that she has experienced much anguish before arriving at this stage. Fortunately, she has an older brother who "broke the ice." The emotional costs are heavy, however, sometimes resulting in confusion and depression, which she tells us her brother experiences. It is much easier when the family or a group of families leaves together.

Barbara's sister, whom we meet later, describes her as confident, buoyant, and optimistic. She revels in each new day and anticipates the challenges that await her. Perhaps some of her strength comes from her leaving for spiritual rather than for material reasons.

For those persons who are born Amish and who can accept the constraints of their society, life is both fulfilling and secure. Barbara, however, represents those individuals who, despite having been reared in loving Amish homes, have felt stifled. Try as they might, they find it too hard to blend into the patchwork of Amish culture.

They do not fit the pattern.

Do Chickens Come Home
to Roost?

I awaken this Sunday morning about dawn in the upstairs bedroom in the house of the Amish couple with whom we will be attending church. The sounds of laughter and the conversations of male and female voices drift through the walls of the adjoining bedroom. I am surprised that John and Rebecca, the husband and wife with whom we are staying, are so lively this early in the morning. Then I remember that their bedroom is downstairs and realize that this must be the bedroom of their youngest son, Andy, the only one of their five children who still lives at home.

But who is the female with him and when did she get there? Is she Amish or English? Is Andy aware that we are staying with his parents? He was not home when we arrived last night. Do Rebecca and John know this girl or woman is here? Because the four of us will leave soon after breakfast for the church service in a house several miles away, they may never know that she is here—or that we know about her presence. While the custom of bed courtship, or "bundling," as it is commonly called, is still practiced in some Amish settlements, it is traditionally the young man who goes to the home of the young woman; and the presence of a young woman in the bedroom of a young male in an Amish home is certainly suspect. As my husband and I rise and dress, talking aloud and walking around the room, the activity in Andy's room subsides to silence, as though the voices we heard were our own ghostly imaginings or echoes from our half-forgotten dreams.

John and Rebecca have told us of the heartbreak Andy has caused them ever since he apparently rejected the Amish way of life at age eighteen. Although a period of *Rumspringa*, "running around," is the norm for Amish youth, Andy has gone beyond the typical Rumspringa behavior, which often includes owning or riding in cars, dressing in English clothes, and participating in the "hops" or hoedowns where alcohol flows freely. One Amish minister admitted that during his Rumspringa he not only owned a car but also took flying lessons.

Since the Amish consider the taking of the vows of church membership akin to taking the vows of marriage, and since serious deviation from the Ordnung will result in shunning once a person has "joined church," Amish young folk sometimes use this Rumspringa period as a means of experiencing English society before settling down and committing to the Amish way of life. In fact, some—but by no means all—older Amish believe that the youth will be better church members for having "gotten it out of their system." Those who take this stance say, "Let them alone and they will come back."

Usually Amish youth who engage in such behavior do it together. That is, they may be "bad" Amish while they are breaking the rules, but they are still Amish—even if not officially. However, when a young person "runs around" with English friends, parents who might otherwise avert their eyes and wait for their youth to get safely over "fools' hill" become alarmed. They fear that if their young people imbibe too much of English society, they might not return to the fold to become stalwart, devout, rule-abiding members of the community. Some families tell tales of apostate relatives who have slipped into very un-Amish lifestyles that include drunkenness, drugs, and divorce. These stories are related by parents and ministers as a warning to the youth of the possible results of abandoning their faith.

Not infrequently, segments of the youth group in some of the larger settlements engage in such rowdy activities at the singings that non-Amish neighbors call the police to break them up. Sometimes local authorities require young persons from Amish homes who have been caught driving under the influence of alcohol to attend special classes. This attracts the attention of the surrounding English community, as a succession of articles in the local newspapers in one county attests: "Police Raid Farm Hoedown," "Three Charged with Drinking," "Noisy Nights," "Cars Stolen from Amish Youth," "Seven Arrested, Fifty Scatter."[1] As a result of these excesses, some Amish parents will not allow youth to congregate at their houses or barns. Such is the case in the settlement in which Andy grew up.

John and Rebecca can identify the exact point at which Andy's rebellion became serious: John had broken up an unapproved gathering that Andy had arranged at their house, a wild party that was overrun by youth from other districts in an adjoining county. Angry at his father's

---

1. These newspaper headlines are from the *Lancaster Intelligencer Journal* and the *Lancaster New Era*.

action, Andy deliberately took all his money and left home to live with English friends, returning several months later "filthy and penniless," John reports.

"Of course we took him in," John tells us. "How could any caring parent do otherwise?"

This may sound like the parable of the prodigal son, but so far Andy has failed to exhibit the repentance depicted in the biblical account. The pickup truck parked behind the barn evidences his continuing deviant Rumspringa behavior. Its presence means that not only does Andy incur the disapproval of the church community, but so do John and Rebecca, since they allow him to keep it there. John defends their decision, expressing his fears regarding where Andy might be if they forbid him to do so. They don't want to act too drastically after what happened the first time.

Meanwhile, Andy is exhibiting other behavioral patterns that have caused his parents to worry. He has been very rude to Rebecca recently, demanding that she prepare his lunches to his specifications and expressing no gratitude for her compliance. Also, John worries about Andy's close association with non-Amish coworkers in the trailer factory where he is employed, but most especially about his association with non-Amish girls, among them an English girl and a "black-bumper" Mennonite. (The conservative Horning Mennonites drive black cars with the black bumpers, hence the nickname "black-bumper" Mennonite). We understand his concern, since often Amish youth who associate with conservative Mennonite groups, most notably the "black-bumper" Mennonites and Beachy Amish churches, appear to be more likely to leave the Old Order fold than those who have a brief "fling" with wildness. Parents fear that contact with young people of less strict persuasion will cause them to question the whole Amish system. Of course, the association with an English girl also has its dangers. Very few English girls can meet the expectations put on Amish wives, and the cultures are so far apart that divorces are more likely to result in such matches.

News of Andy's behavior has caused some fathers in the settlement to caution their daughters about their association with him. Only recently the father of Andy's Amish girlfriend has forbidden her to see him. John thinks Andy has not yet recovered from this blow, remarking that very often the young women in the community keep the guys from truly wild behavior, and that now this safeguard has been taken away from Andy. And finally, John confides as we pull into the lane of the house where service will be held this morning, Andy has been to church only half a dozen times in the last year.

To our surprise, he is there this morning. Only his stylishly feathered haircut signals his deviance; his dress and deportment would never lead the casual observer to question his commitment to the Amish way of life. He sits quietly on the bench with bowed head, like most of his friends, and, like them, does not enter into the singing. He greets us shyly after the service, never letting on that we might have heard some things he would rather we hadn't earlier that morning. But he does not stay for the shared meal after church, disappearing like most of the older teenage males into the barn to harness his horse and carriage, which he reserves for Sunday services only.

Across the ensuing weeks and months John updates us on Andy's progress—or the lack thereof. He reports that Rebecca found a half-filled bottle of whiskey under Andy's bed, which she promptly replaced with water. John had to break up another party that Andy hosted at their house. The youth had supposedly gathered for a singing, but it turned out to be only a ruse for getting everyone together, John explains. John and an English neighbor confiscated several six-packs of beer, took them in John's buggy, and dumped them over a bank where the youth could not find them. Later the group ransacked John's carriage, overturning the seats but causing no serious damage. Andy, of course, was furious with his father. While John does not say so, he probably fears that Andy might leave again as he had the first time John broke up one of Andy's parties.

To our surprise, Andy has begun dating Sarah, the deacon's daughter, but so far it hasn't produced any apparent change in his behavior. John approves of Sarah. He informs us that pregnancies are more likely to result when the girls join in the drinking but adds that Sarah isn't that kind of girl. Still, John wonders how Sarah tolerates the figure of a naked woman that Andy has dangling from the mirror in his truck and the figures of busty females on the mud flaps. What does Sarah see in him? This romance seems incongruous to outside eyes.

"Why does Sarah let him get away with that? She should be acting as a restraint," John insists.

Rebecca asserts that Sarah is a restraint. Considering that possibility, John speculates that maybe one of the reasons why Andy gets really angry is that Sarah may be nagging him about his behavior. He also believes that when Andy is with his English friends, they have a TV and VCR in the room and that they watch pornographic movies together. The lines on his forehead and the tension in his voice reveal his deep concern, and he runs his hands down the side of his face and tugs again at his beard.

More months pass, and again my husband is privy to an update on Andy's progress. Andy has reached the age when he should join church, but he still wants to continue playing softball in a league with English youth, so he has declined to become part of the membership class this year. John and Rebecca will not take communion this time because of his actions and their refusal to demand that he not park his truck on their property. Since communion is a solemn occasion held only twice a year, to abstain from participation is a serious act. After three times of missing communion, a member will be put out of the church, but a person cannot conscientiously take communion when things are not right in his or her personal life or household. John says he and Rebecca are in a double bind. And the minister's harping at the congregation for the parking of vehicles on their property isn't doing any good, John asserts. If Andy would park his truck somewhere else and always dress Amish, they would be accepted, but as it is, people don't come to visit them. He knows Andy dresses English sometimes, but what can he and Rebecca do? They don't want to drive him away completely. My husband expresses his sympathy for their situation.

John confides that some of the Amish youth are rumored to be using drugs, although he doesn't know which drugs or their source. He thinks their English neighbor could supply drugs to Andy if he wanted some, since he and Rebecca have counted as many as fifteen cars per night stopping at that house. He doesn't say whether or not he thinks Andy is on drugs, and we don't ask.

The media has recently featured stories of two young men raised in Amish homes being part of a drug bust in the Lancaster County, Pennsylvania, settlement—news which catapulted the Amish community into prominence not only in this country but in other countries as well. Probably few of the admiring tourists who drive along the quiet back roads would have suspected that Amish youth would be guilty of selling and doing drugs. Upon hearing the news, many people expressed dismay that this supposed bastion of virtue has been conquered. But some of the leaders in the settlement and English authorities close to it know that drugs have been around at least since the 1960s. Several years before this drug bust, we listened to a now devout Amishman confess his involvement with drugs during his own wayward years. Of course, his own children would never suspect—and he is wise enough to find ways of keeping them away from situations where they might be tempted to try them. But no parent, English or Amish, can insulate a child completely from exposure to drugs.

Meanwhile, Andy is still playing softball, a sport at which he is proficient, which continues to place him in close contact with English youth. The ruling of the bishops that mothers may not launder the softball uniforms of their wayward sons is complicating matters, John declares. He seems proud of Andy's athletic prowess, despite its being looked down on in the Amish community. He relates that one of the Amish softball teams even traveled to California to play in a tournament.

Softball season passes and fall comes and goes, and still Andy exhibits no evidence of a change of heart. John remarks that he and Sarah seem to be getting along very well and that when he and Rebecca observed Sarah helping to prepare the after-service meal at her family's house, they were impressed by her industriousness. Few qualities are valued more highly in Amish society.

"She's shy, but she's a real worker," he declares. "She and Andy make a good-looking couple, but I don't know what will happen if Andy continues to keep his truck and play softball. Rebecca has urged him to be at least some kind of a church member rather than nothing at all. And I'm afraid the deacon will try to put an end to their courtship if Andy doesn't change soon." Again the worry lines appear on his forehead. What can we say?

More months pass, nothing changes, and we wonder if Andy will eventually leave the Amish way. Then one day John has a new angle to report. "Andy has marriage on his mind," John states. "I think he's sorry he didn't go to the membership classes last spring and then join church in the fall."

Marriage on his mind? If Andy has marriage on his mind, that has serious implications beyond the taking of wedding vows. It means that Andy will have to give up his truck, softball, and his wild English associates. Beginning in June, he will have to take instruction classes held by the bishop and ministers during the early part of the Sunday services. By the third instruction class period he will have to conform to his district's Ordnung or he will not be allowed to continue instruction. If he does complete instruction and if the bishop and ministers are satisfied that he is serious in his intent, he will be allowed to join church in September, taking his lifetime vows. Only then will he and Sarah, who is already a church member, be permitted to marry.

Will the pull of a young woman's love be strong enough to motivate him to give up his English amenities and worldly behavior? It is still several months before the June instruction classes begin. In some Amish settlements the bishops discourage taking instruction classes in the spring and joining church in the fall if the apparent motivation is to marry an Amish girl a few months later. Will that be the case here?

We wait—if not with bated breath, at least with hearty curiosity—knowing that if Andy really has marriage on his mind, it will be the answer to his parents' prayers. Something within me doubts that it will happen—it sounds too much like a saccharine, formula-based piece of fiction. Boy meets girl, boy woos girl, boy wins girl, and boy and girl conquer all obstacles. Or, from another angle, parents face disappointment with erring children, parents hold steady, defying the conventional wisdom of their peers, and behold: their patient love triumphs!

We wait for further unfolding of the story. John, its narrator, merely reports more of the same: "Andy still has marriage on his mind."

Despite my skepticism, the unraveling of the plot occurs quickly and without any complications. A few months later, Andy goes to the first instruction class. By the second one he has sold the truck. By the third one he has expunged himself of all things non-Amish. He's on his way in. I am incredulous.

Not all Amish parents are so fortunate in having events turn out this well. Even as we observe Andy's progress, we hear sad news about young people from another district who had been undergoing similar instruction. Some of them met for one last fling on a weekend night before their third instruction class. A wild car ride and a serious accident left three of the four riders injured and one dead.

John's next installment reveals that Andy has purchased property on which to build a house and that he and Sarah have set their wedding date. In due time, the wedding takes place and following it, the couple live at Sarah's parents' house. By spring their own house is readied and they move in. A real live fairy tale, I decide. Will they now live happily ever after?

My observations of Andy's foray into waywardness and his eventual return to the Amish fold have left me with more questions than answers. What about Amish life is so satisfying that the allurements of the outside world—freedom, individuality, and all the gadgets and conveniences that modern technology offers—fail to convince them that they should abandon their simple, community-based way of life? Do Amish persons who have dabbled in and then rejected English society become more committed to their own values as a result of their experiences, having once and for all dealt with their wanderlust and worked it "out of their system?" And finally, has Andy really changed, or is he merely outwardly observant?

He has mingled with some of the less admirable members of English society, including a number of individuals whom many English parents would not want their sons and daughters to be associated with. He has also glimpsed what it would be like to be free of the constraints that are placed on him by his culture. Yet he has turned his back on English culture and returned to a way of life that, despite its assets, appears quaint, often legalistic, and impossibly out-of-date.

Or is it? Is it just possible that community, simplicity, and faith—and a sense of definite boundaries—are the enduring values that give life meaning and that he has found mainstream American society deficient in these elements? Perhaps Wallace Stegner's words, although written in a different context, apply here as well: "American individualism, much celebrated and cherished, has developed without its essential corrective, which is belonging. Freedom, when found, can turn out to be airless and unsustaining."[2] When questioned about the sudden shift from waywardness to compliance with the rigid demands of the church which some Amish youth experience, one young man in his early twenties rejoined, "It's not at all hard to cut off worldly behavior immediately and get into line. In some ways it's a relief. You know what's expected of you, and you have a place where you fit." As a popular Amish axiom declares, "Chickens come home to roost," and they mean this in a positive light, rather than in the negative sense in which it is often quoted in English society.

Andy's story is not at all unusual; we have heard similar tales about men and women who are now stalwart patriarchs and matriarchs in their churches. But now we have observed for ourselves a prodigal's return. Still we are left with the question: Why did he come back?

2. Wallace Stegner, *Where the Bluebird Sings to the Lemonade Springs* (1992; rpt., New York: Wing Books, 1995), 72.

10

When Death Comes

Steven S. King: May 18, 1977–June 21, 1994

Bad news does indeed travel quickly. A phone call informs us that an Amish family we admire so much has been shattered by the drowning of their second oldest son. Shocked, we try to absorb the details surrounding his death and endeavor to respond to the family's sorrow.

Steven King[1] is dead at age seventeen years and one month. Never do our souls rebel against death more than at the death of the young and the good. Steven King was both. He is mourned by his parents, nine brothers and sisters, and other relatives and friends, most of them Old Order Amish.

We enter the long farm lane in this distant corner of Lancaster County, Pennsylvania, far from the prying eyes of the tourists who crowd the garish strips along Route 30. The clear light of the June evening and the verdant growth of the crops around us cry out against our reason for coming. Conspicuous in our English clothing, we make our way among the stream of gray carriages and dark horses, among the congregating somber figures, some of them transported to the home of Steven's family in vans now parked obtrusively in the alfalfa field.

Every Amish man and woman is garbed in black, silent and deliberate, moving among the crunching of wheels upon gravel toward the house. Hundreds have come, a community of support gathering to press the hands of the family and of each other, to mourn, to accept, to try to understand. In hushed tones they exchange the details—the fateful activities at the pond, the rush to the hospital, the coma, the respirator, the flat brain waves. Then came the unplugging, the tears and the prayers, the good-bye kisses, every member of the family present.

Young Steven King died on the first day of summer, 1994.

1. This is the only instance in the book where the name of the person has not been changed. The details of this sorrowful occasion are as I remember them.

On rows of benches crowded in the kitchen, sitting room, and parlor sit the silent friends and acquaintances who have come to show they care. We move in a line toward the center, shaking strong hands as we pass. We enter the bedroom of Steven's parents, the room of conception and birth—and now of death—bare except for the six-sided casket with its coverlet of white cloth. In it lies the shell that was Steven.

A respectful and obedient son, he took over many of the farm tasks when his father was chosen bishop, to give his father more time to fulfill his responsibilities. During a recent Sunday service he led the singing of the Amish praise hymn, "Lob Lied," an act usually reserved for older men. Only a few days ago he had refused to drink alcoholic beverages when pressured by some young men in the community. Looking at his sallow face, we strain to accept what we long to deny.

In the parlor the parents sit, not as host and hostess ministering to their guests, but as recipients of the ministrations of their friends. One by one with soft words and stout handshakes they greet the family, then linger to talk quietly with each other. The faces of his parents appear gaunt and strained, yet strong and composed. We mumble our inadequate expressions of sympathy and promises of prayer.

The father's response is one of faith and assurance, of trust in the God who knows best, who gives strength to those who trust his purposes. The mother speaks of acceptance, of confidence in knowing that Steven is happy in the presence of God. They are glad we have come.

So are we, having been comforted by looking into the many faces and participated briefly in that community of faith, by sharing this unfathomable sorrow, by observing the manner in which the family is persevering.

Outside the full moon rises above the full fields. We hesitate to enjoy the hushed beauty, as though doing so might be disrespectful to the dead and the grieving. In the midst of life, I muse, there is death.

Then I recall the words of Quaker poet John Greenleaf Whittier—words the Amish mourners would approve: "I know not what the future hath / Of marvel or surprise, / Assured alone that life and death / His mercy underlies."[2] We drive away into the soft light of evening. In the midst of death there is life.

---

2. John Greenleaf Whittier, "The Eternal Goodness." *The Complete Poetical Works of John Greenleaf Whittier* (Boston: Houghton Mifflin, 1884), 231.

11

On the Move

I do not want to stop and visit. Already travel-weary, I want to push on to our destination a few hours away. Besides, I point out to my husband, since it is about five o'clock, the family may be eating supper. According to my upbringing, one does not arrive unannounced at mealtime, especially if one hasn't already eaten. Also, it isn't as though they are old friends, I argue. We've only been here once before, I remind him, and then we were introduced to them by another Amish couple from the settlement where they had formerly lived.

But he presses me, and soon we are trudging across the stone walkway to the back porch of the aging turn-of-the-century farmhouse, its peeling paint an obvious contrast to the neat farm complexes where the owners previously lived. An Amishwoman in a plain gray dress and prim white head covering appears in the door. Affable and personable as ever, my husband reintroduces himself. She nods and smiles, passing her hand across her skirt in a gentle caress, and I realize she is pregnant.

"Eli is finishing the milking in the barn," she informs me, "but he and the older boys should be back in a little while. Won't you come in?"

We enter the dim kitchen, lighted only by the lamp and warmed by the huge, black cook stove on this windy December evening. The chipped enamel sink, tall outdated cupboards, worn counters, and faded linoleum suggest that little in the room has been altered since the house was built. Crowded into one corner is an oval table still cluttered with soup plates, plastic cups, scattered silver, bread crumbs, and other bits of food. A year-old baby sits in a wooden high chair, whimpering slightly at the sight of strangers.

"Have you eaten?" she asks, and we admit that we have not. "Would you like some stew?" she queries, gathering up a pile of dirty dishes in one sweep with as welcoming a smile as though we were long-awaited relatives from a distant state. I note the two-quart jar half-full of meat on the counter, probably used in the vegetable stew she is offering, and hope that it was pressure-canned and botulism free. I wish that I weren't so squeamish about such things.

The stew and the bread are both delicious, and so is the homemade bologna. Two little girls come into the kitchen and shyly hide behind their mother's skirt until she insists that they say hello to the "company." The baby in the high chair is not a girl, she tells us, although attired in a dress. I have seen other Amish baby boys dressed in this way and wonder about the custom: easier to change the diapers, maybe, since possibly the Amish in this settlement do not use the snap-up one-piece sleepers so popular now?

While my husband goes out to join Eli in the barn, I wash the dishes, trying to make conversation. She is not inhibited by non-Amish people. Perhaps this is partly because she has siblings who are not Amish. She talks freely about them, which is not always the case; sometimes Amish prefer to keep quiet about family members who have defected from the faith.

"How long have you lived here?" I ask.

"We moved a year ago in March," she replies. "We wanted to get away from the negative influences in the other settlement, and this one seemed like a good place. But the weather out here is pretty severe; we have about six weeks less growing season than we had before. So it hasn't been easy. Still, we're glad we made the move. The older boys [ages nine and eleven] love the farm and the out-of-doors, and we're more in accord with the ways of this district. It's a better place to raise children," she continues. "Our nearest Amish neighbors are less than a mile away, and the non-Amish neighbors nearby are friendly. That helps."

Five—soon to be six—children to take care of, and no grandpas, grand-mas, uncles, or aunties to help, I muse. A run-down farm and house not nearly so spacious as the Amish houses I know—and probably not well insulated, either. How can she be so cheerful and hospitable, I wonder, with so much work to do and so few conveniences?

The stomping of feet on the porch signals the arrival of Eli, their sons, and my husband; and their chatter and laughter suggest they are getting along well. After further greetings, everyone gathers in the sitting room to talk. The little girls cuddle against their oldest brother on the couch who turns the pages of a picture book for them, listening at the same time to the conversation his parents are carrying on with us. In the rocking chair, Rachel sits with the baby contentedly sucking his thumb on her lap. The remaining boy climbs onto his father's knee and strokes his beard. Rachel passes some pretzels and freshly baked chocolate chip cookies.

The baby fusses and Rachel pats him absentmindedly. I should be so laid-back, I think—laid-back enough to welcome unannounced guests warmly despite a messy house and all the work involved in rearing young children. And I know this is not unusual—her guest book is bulging with the names of visitors. Already they have asked us to stay overnight, even though it means the older boys will have to sleep in their parents' room. Since we have no deadline to meet, we accept.

They share their story with us. They have moved to this county because her husband was troubled by the inconsistencies between his stated beliefs and his actual lifestyle. He had found ways to "cheat" on the Amish rules—to appear on the surface to be an upstanding member of the Amish community while actually engaging in practices forbidden by the local Ordnung. Realizing that his life lacked integrity, he decided to make the necessary changes. His wife supported his decision and submissively joined him in the move across the state. Here in this settlement, he believes the atmosphere is more conducive to living out his Christian faith. If it isn't, they will move again.

Their decision has proven to be more costly than they had anticipated, however. Their first year was difficult because the farm was more run-down than they had realized, but they have no regrets. Their oldest son, a bright and outgoing sixth-grader, expresses his pleasure at living on the farm near a wooded area and can't imagine living anywhere else. I sense a peace—a genuine contentment—among them that is enviable.

Old Order Amish families do not have the same freedom to choose where they will attend church that people who identify with other denominations have. If they live in a certain geographical district, they must attend the services that are held within that district, except for occasional visits to other districts or those of friends and relatives. They cannot choose to become members of a neighboring district because they prefer the ministers or bishop or feel more "at home" there.

When they disagree with the beliefs or practices of the district in which they live, they may occasionally leave the Old Order Church and join a "higher" group, such as the New Order or a Beachy Amish group. However, this can mean cutting ties with family and friends, and, depending on the Ordnung of the local district, it can also mean being shunned. Shunning for leaving and joining a "higher" Amish group is more common in Lancaster County, Pennsylvania, than in Holmes County, Ohio, where some Amish persons have been accused of "stepping" their way "up and out." Since in Holmes County it is not unusual for a person or family to join the next higher group without being shunned, often a person can work his way from being Old Order Amish, to New Order Amish, to Beachy or conservative Mennonite, to the Mennonite Church without experiencing the severe treatment that one would receive if he joined a Mennonite Church directly upon leaving his Old Order Amish district.

But in many other localities, when people become unhappy enough with conditions in their local district, they may choose to move to another Old Order settlement. Sometimes the reasons for moving are very practical. A group of families may start a new settlement because of crowding in their previous district, because land has become too expensive for them to purchase additional tracts for younger couples, or because the land is not productive enough for them to support their families.

In some instances, individuals or families will migrate because of social concerns, religious convictions, or a combination of these. Couples with children approaching their teenage years may move because they view the youth of their present district as too wild and they do not want their children to associate with them. Or they may move if they believe their church district is more concerned with tradition than with truly "spiritual" concerns, especially if they claim to have experienced a genuine conversion but live in a district where most members look down on "revivalism." Sometimes the motivation is discomfort with particular aspects of the Ordnung, which they find either more strict or more liberal than they like. We have learned, however, that the stated reason is only part of the motivation for moving, and often the real impetus for leaving may have more to do with personality conflicts than with the productivity of the land or personal convictions.

Whatever the reason for moving, Amish persons must take into consideration whether they are willing to adjust to the Ordnung of the new settlement. Some of the adjustments Eli and Rachel have had to make are evident to us since we are familiar with their home district. Rachel's "dress code" is plainer, and she must use a coal stove in her kitchen rather than a gas one. Since she cannot have a gas refrigerator (of course an electric one is forbidden), Eli has found a way to power one by diverting energy from the diesel engine that keeps the milk cool.

Since Eli and Rachel moved primarily because of spiritual concerns, they have been willing to make the adjustments. I sense Rachel's strength and contentment as well as a quiet confidence. She appears to know who she is and what she is about, whereas at times I feel that I have spent half a lifetime trying to answer those questions. She is wife and mother, second only to child of God. The former two she assumes as a matter of course since they are the roles almost all Amishwomen aspire to, but she talks freely about the latter in words that more closely resemble a born-again evangelical Christian than an ethnic Amish. When my husband describes an Amish settlement in the Midwest that is even plainer than the Nebraska and the Swartzentruber Amish communities, her immediate response is, "Yes, but what is their Christianity like?" I wonder if other members in her new church district share her views of spirituality.

Like all Amish persons, Eli and Rachel are aware of the variations in Amish settlements. Rumors circulate through the scattered communities regarding which districts cannot restrain their youth from holding wild parties, which ones have high rates of premarital pregnancies, and which supposedly are having power conflicts. The Amish grapevine is efficient enough to communicate these and more subtle differences across the miles.

Later I query my husband on the frequency of such moving about: Is it more common now than in past decades? I enumerate a half-dozen families I know who have either moved or will be moving soon. Well, he replies, there have always been the mavericks among the Amish who have moved out beyond the confines of the larger settlements and have taken followers with them. Individual families have moved, too. How else does one account for settlements in Texas, Montana, and the now extinct one in Oregon?

In the morning I apologize to my husband for my reluctance to stop to visit with Eli and Rachel. We have been blessed by our brief stay. Their prioritizing of the spiritual well-being of themselves and their family above material comforts has challenged us to examine our own practices. Since Eli and Rachel live along a route we travel to see relatives, we often visit their family, as well and find ourselves enriched by their friendship. We are equally pleased when they stop for lunch at our house with their children on their way to a family gathering. We watch as another child, and yet another, are added to their brood.

Then along with a Christmas card comes news that we had heard from mutual friends but which is now confirmed in writing. We will not be able to stop again at their house to hear the laughter of their children and to chat with them about what is happening in their lives. They have sold their cows. Their farm equipment will be auctioned off at a sale in the near future. They do not tell us directly, but we know from hints dropped in previous conversations that the difficult farming situation coupled with the church district's legalism and stress on tradition have led to disillusionment with their location. They are moving again to a settlement known for its emphasis on personal salvation. We hope we will not lose touch.

12

On Punishment and Prodigals

$\mathcal{S}$traight out of a Dickens novel he appears with my husband at our front door, younger and much more confident than Bob Cratchit, merry as old Mr. Fezziwig, and more robust. Dressed in a soft wool greatcoat with a dignified cape, his dark hair curling from beneath his black, broad-brimmed felt hat, his red-cheeked smile punctuated by a dimple in his chin, he seems bigger than life, like one of the nineteenth-century fictional characters he resembles.

The young man belongs to one of the Old Order horse-and-buggy Mennonite sects that are similar to their Amish neighbors, resembling them in faith and practice much as first cousins favor each other, yet he is different in both physical appearance and bearing from any Amishman I can think of. Perhaps it is the absence of a beard. His clean-shaven face and his bright blue-green shirt appear startlingly incongruous against his plain black coat and broad-fall trousers. Usually Amishmen don't dress in such bright colors.

But no—it is more than that, I decide. Something in the way he carries himself and in his eagerness to articulate his ideas is foreign to the plain manner I usually associate with the Amish. I wonder if he knows the term Gelassenheit and soon conclude that while his self-confidence is far from pride or even self-consciousness, he does not conduct himself with the self-effacing hesitancy I have come to expect from many members of the Amish groups I know.

Soon he is sitting at our dinner table engaged in an exchange with my husband concerning the practices of his church and explaining why *Mei-dung* (shunning) is both necessary and effective in the life of a genuine Anabaptist community. Shunning is the practice of severely limiting social and business contacts with an Amish church member who has broken either the church rules or his or her vow to stay with the church till death. Members are placed under this "ban" only when they are still unrepentant after having been approached by church leaders about their behavior.

While specifics vary from settlement to settlement, in many Amish groups shunning includes not eating at the same table with church members, even with relatives; not being directly involved in business transactions; and, in its most severe form, forbidding husband and wife to engage in sexual relations. Such ostracism is often effective in bringing about the desired repentance among the community-based Anabaptists, who suffer from the severing of social and emotional connections. Sometimes, however, it works the other way and drives the wayward church member completely from the fold and into another church or even apostasy. Still, I can't ignore the comment of one observer who pointed out that one shouldn't be too harsh in criticizing "a 300-year-old practice that often seems to work better than [the more lenient practices of a modern Anabaptist denomination] where anything goes." Maybe so, but the practice of shunning has been a divisive issue among the Amish since their inception.

Shunning, our guest declares, is very scriptural. I ponder the passages he refers me to. St. Paul counsels, "But now I am writing you that you must not associate with anyone who calls himself a brother but is sexually immoral or greedy, an idolater or a slanderer, a drunkard or a swindler. With such a man do not even eat. What business is it of mine to judge those outside the church? Are you not to judge those inside? God will judge those outside. 'Expel the wicked man from among you'" (I Corinthians 5: 11–12, NIV).

Just as significant is another passage cited in most Anabaptist denominations, Matthew 18. In that chapter Jesus discusses what to do when "a brother sins against you." "Go and show him his fault, just between the two of you," instructs Jesus. "If he listens to you, you have won your brother over. But if he will not listen, take one or two others along, so that every matter may be established by the testimony of two or three witnesses. If he refuses to listen to them, tell it to the church, and if he refuses to listen even to the church, treat him as you would a pagan or a tax collector" (Matthew 18: 15–17, NIV). To say the least, it sounds like very tough love. Of course other scriptural passages would imply less severe treatment of the wayward. What should Christians do when individuals or groups assign different weights to scriptural passages that seem to be in opposition to each other, I wonder.

Had we noticed, our friend continues, that church members who abandon shunning eventually leave the old Anabaptist ways and join another less demanding group?

Is that so bad, I want to ask. Is any one person or group capable of interpreting the will of God so precisely that he or she can afford to stand in judgment of another human being on such minutiae as sleeve length, beard length—or shirt color, I think, glancing again at his shirt. One Beachy Amishman thinks that probably 70 percent of his Old Order neighbors would prefer to use tractors if the truth were known, but they will not go against the local Ordnung. Often it isn't the particular issue that matters most; it is the willingness to submit to the standards agreed upon by the group. Of course, the outward keeping of the law does not mean the inward assent, especially in a community where the consequences of dissent are so severe.

I recall the often repeated story of the little girl who, when forced by a parent to sit down, retorted, "Okay, but on the inside I'm still standing up." How many plain folk who keep the rules do so out of humble submission and conviction, how many out of an unexamined acceptance of tradition, and how many merely because of the devastating social ostracism they would experience if they did otherwise? Maybe inside they are still "standing up." Of course we would both agree that only God can judge the intent of the heart.

Perhaps if shunning were limited to the sins mentioned in the Corinthians 5 passages—sexual immorality, greed, idolatry, slandering, drunkenness, and swindling—the practice would be more tolerable to outsiders. If one believes that a loved one or a church member is bound for hell because of his or her actions, then shunning makes a lot of sense. And, in truth, shunning is most often reserved for "real" sins such as leaving the faith, which is a violation of one's church vows; defrauding others; and sexual immorality. But not always. Of course, I do not tell my guest these thoughts. Mostly I listen and observe.

But shunning must be carried out in love, of course, he asserts, if it is to be effective.

Maybe so, replies my husband. But often it isn't. The custom is one of the most exasperating Amish and Old Order Mennonite practices to outsiders, who see it as both unreasonable and cruel, my husband remarks. He adds that certain Amish groups in the Midwest practice a very limited kind of shunning, some observing it for only a few months.

And how effective can that kind of shunning be, our guest asks. If a person knows that banishment from interaction with family and friends will be enforced for only a few months, he can hold out for that long. How will that help him to see the error of his ways? How will he be brought to a state of repentance and restoration? How will he see what it means to be cut off from the community of righteousness? What really is accomplished by a temporary shunning?

He is very perceptive and articulate, I observe as I bring out the pie and coffee. And logically he may be correct. I think of a recently married Old Order Amish couple who were shunned for a mere six weeks when the church leaders eventually discovered that the bride was already pregnant before the couple was married. In addition, they had lied to the ministers and deacons regarding their having sexual relations. The couple knew that they would ultimately be forgiven and restored into the circle of family and community. This kind of behavior, according to one Amish person, is not uncommon, pointing out the couple experience not only confession and humiliation, but also relief: "It's out! Over. I'm forgiven." Maybe it's the Amish version of Roman Catholic penance.

One Amish family shunned their daughter when she revealed that she was planning to marry a man who was a member of a relatively plain Amish Mennonite group that allows its members to drive cars. Their shunning did not prevent the marriage, but it did cause a lot of stress in the relationships between family members, so much that rumors circulated that the mother was on the verge of a "nervous breakdown." Later I watched a relative of the daughter who had left arrange the breakfast table so that, even though food was placed upon it and we sat around it, technically it was not "set" for a meal. Perhaps it was her way of expressing disapproval while keeping the letter of the law and still not rejecting her relative. Many families accomplish this by placing a smaller table a few inches away from the larger table and having the shunned family members eat separately or with the children or unbaptized youth.

A former Amishman recalls how many years ago he left the Old Order group for the less conservative Beachy Amish group because he reasoned that since he was riding in other people's cars, he ought to be able to purchase and drive one. What he *used*, he asserted, logically he should be permitted to *own*. He was excommunicated for this action and for refusing to condemn a fellow Amishman who owned a car, but he was not placed "in the ban,"—the Amish term for shunning—a most unusual situation. Forty years later, however, another Amishman in a distant settlement would still not invite him into his home.

Sometimes the shunning can involve a group. The ministers in one Amish church district decided to leave and form their own church district. Had they held a service before the main group had time to meet and to place them "under the ban," they would not have been shunned. However, time did not allow for that, so rather than being considered a legitimate separate church district, now they are treated as outcasts. Such hairsplitting seems ludicrous to outsiders, and must surely drive away nonbelievers who might otherwise be impressed with the seriousness with which the Amish attempt to live out their faith.

We have listened to parents express their pain because of their own possible excommunication since their wayward son still lives at home and they have refused to put him out or to demand that he not park his truck on their property. They wonder if their yielding to the dictates of the church regarding these issues would be a kind of "tough love" that will show him how seriously they take their religious commitments and thus draw him back, or if it would ultimately seem to him a cruel legalism that drives him away. How must it feel not to be able to eat at the same table with a son or daughter or sister or brother because they have refused to follow the rules of the church?

Still, I am forced to admit that much too often, modern churches close their eyes when members continue in transgressions that are blatant and in direct opposition to both Scripture and their vows to their church. Sometimes serious sins that are unspeakably detrimental to those against whom they are committed are swept under the rug. And many church members would likely resent questioning or rebuking by one of their fellow church members. Nor would they tolerate any action remotely resembling shunning; they would simply change churches, choosing to fellowship with a group of believers who agreed with them.

So often the scriptures force believers to hold two opposing concepts in tension. Somehow they must reconcile St. Paul's commands and Amish shunning practices with the New Testament assertions that judgment and vengeance are not theirs to wield but God's, while still recognizing that they are "our brothers and sisters' keepers." Is there a kind of balance that eludes Amish and English alike?

Earlier this evening our guest had shared the news of his still secret engagement; he is to be married in about three months. I wonder what he knows about wayward children? How will he and his wife feel someday if one of their children does not embrace their way of life and join their church? Or—worse still—if a child of theirs joins the church and then leaves it?

I do know what it feels like to have a child reject the faith.

One particular chapter in the Bible has been of more comfort to me in this matter than any other. It does not tell me what to do. It says nothing—pro or con—about the matter of shunning. Nor is it a reasoned treatise on any organized doctrine.

In Luke 15, Jesus tells a series of three stories about three lost and found items: a lost sheep, a lost coin, and a lost child. Often I have pondered the similarities and differences among these stories, between the God figure in each and the differences in the way in which the lost item is found by that God figure. Sometimes the God figure searches, sometimes He waits. In the third story it is, ironically, the other son—the legalistic but unforgiving, rule-keeping son—whom the God figure seeks. Some Bible commentators aren't at all convinced that the "prodigal" in that story came home for the right reasons. I don't understand it all, but I am comforted. And I am convinced that whatever the particular techniques, it is love that wins. Perhaps our guest already knows this, but if not he will learn it in the crucible of life.

We are both twenty-first-century Anabaptists, but with marked distinctions. I dress in contemporary styles, not at all like the Old Order groups; our Anabaptist guest wears the traditional plain clothing handed down from his ancestors. I question both tradition and authority; he embraces them. I have been adopted into my Anabaptist denomination; he can trace his heritage through several generations. We shake hands at the door. I express my earnest hope that I will see him again. I wish him and his future wife blessings. We say good-bye.

I hope we are more alike than we are different. I hope our major aim in life is to find God's will—and do it. But I am convinced that all our *doing* will never merit God's *loving*. And the older I get, the more content I am to leave the judging to God.

13

Samuel's Story

We are sitting in the living room of an Ohio Swartzentruber Amish couple in the twilight of a warm August evening. Only the Nebraska Amish in central Pennsylvania's Big Valley are stricter, and only with them and a few other very conservative groups do the Swartzentruber Amish interact closely. My husband and our host converse quietly in the gathering darkness; many Amish put off lighting lamps until they are absolutely necessary. I am grateful that the dimness allows me to peer more easily at my surroundings without seeming unduly curious.

The living room, approximately twenty feet by twelve feet, has a bare wooden floor and glossy white walls with gray wood trim around the doors and windows. A single-paneled black curtain made of coarse fabric is pulled back and tied midway on each window. No pictures of any kind adorn the walls, only a plain calendar with large black numbers marking off the dates. A large black stove with a wooden drying rack above it occupies much of the space against the inside wall between two doors leading to other parts of the house. The furniture consists of worn benches; two rocking chairs, one a rustic rocker made of bent hickory saplings; several straight chairs; a large secretary; a treadle sewing machine; a wash stand; and a rectangular Shaker-like table. Two kerosene lamps rest on the table opposite the stove. Only when it is almost dark does our host rise to light one.

He talks slowly about the customs of this particular settlement, while his more reticent wife sits rocking her chair on the opposite side of the table. Her white cotton prayer covering, which effectively hides all of her hair, has narrow, evenly spaced pleats on the crown, their intricacy contrasting with the plainness of her dress and the starkness of the room itself. When I ask later, she tells me the pleats are set in the fabric by using a table knife.

I wonder how such beauty came to be a part of the regulation dress for women of this the strictest—or, as they would say, "lowest"—of the half-dozen different or so Amish groups in eastern Ohio. The Swartzentruber group split from the Old Order Amish in 1918 over "wanting things more modern"—perhaps more accurately, over *not* wanting things more modern. Or as our host himself remarked regarding the split, "Some say they split from us, and others we split from them."

By their own confession, the Swartzentrubers represent the "plainest of the plain" in dress and hair style. The women wear only the darkest of colors—usually blue, brown, or black—with their dresses reaching to their black shoes, while the men sport longer, blunter haircuts and hats with broader brims than those in most other Amish groups. Their church services are longer—nearly four hours whereas the typical Old Order service lasts around three hours. One reason for this is that the Swartzentrubers sing their hymns at a slower tempo. Their farms, often located on the more remote back roads, typically consist of unadorned white farmhouses with unpainted outbuildings of hodge-podge construction, surrounded by piles of ancient rusting farm implements, cast-off plastic drums, and old lumber. And since they do not use gravel on their lanes, rain and snow can turn them into a muddy mess.

The Swartzentrubers traditionally have used very little machinery of any kind, except for belt-driven equipment powered by two-cycle gasoline engines and chain saws. They rely almost completely on horsepower for their farmwork or do it by hand. In contrast to the Old Order groups nearby, they typically do not use corn pickers or hay bakers, choosing to pick and shell their corn by hand (although this may be changing). They harness horses to power their mowers in the fields, but they use push mowers for the grass nearest their houses. No diesel generators are permitted in the barns for keeping the milk cool or powering any kind of machinery. Hence, all milking is done by hand, often while sitting on three-legged stools. They store the milk in large cans rather than in cooled tanks and thus must sell it as grade B milk for cheese making. And whereas most Amish will hire and ride in cars and vans, the Swartzentrubers traditionally have done so only for emergencies.

Inside the house the same primitive conditions prevail. No plumbing system of any kind exists; instead, many depend on small "kitchen pumps" for their water. The Swartzentrubers do not use refrigerators, unlike many of the "higher" groups whose gas refrigerators look and operate like the electric ones they are forbidden to own. They rely on spring houses or cool cellars, buying ice only for special occasions such as weddings. And since they are not permitted to use natural gas for cooking, they sell the rights to the natural gas on their properties and use

stoves fueled by kerosene. Floors are worn, bare boards except for an occasional throw rug, and the only window adornment is a single curtain
panel, usually dark blue or black, pulled back on a nail during the day
but dropped again in the evening to maintain privacy. As I make my way
to the outhouse, I note that the same austerity exists in the yards, whose
starkness contrasts with the neat, colorful flower gardens that line the
lanes of Lancaster County Amish farms.

Just how aloof they are is demonstrated by their shunning of members
of their group who defect to other Amish groups in their region, even the
conservative Old Order groups. Hence in Ohio they are at the bottom
of the Amish ladder—the least envied, but, because of their quaintness,
perhaps the most interesting. Among the neighboring "higher" Amish
groups and the Mennonite churches, the Swartzentrubers are sometimes regarded as dirty, ignorant, unkempt, and stubborn. Locally they
are sometimes the subject of humorous stories or the butt of jokes.

In some states, settlements of Swartzentruber Amish have resisted
the use of the orange, triangular, slow-moving vehicle sign required by
law. In one state, the group seems ready to accept a compromise, the use
of orange tape placed in a triangular shape rather than the customary
sign. In another state, however, the issue has caused a split, with one
group complying with the law and the other purportedly painting the
sign black—according to rumors circulating among their Old Order and
New Order Amish neighbors. The resistance of the Swartzentrubers is
summed up in the retort they give when questioned about their stance, a
laconic but firm, "It's just our way."

Because of the severe separatist stance and the conservatism of the
Swartzentrubers, other Amish groups often display a fascination for
them, exhibiting a curiosity about their lifestyle and customs much
like the inquisitiveness mainstream Americans have about more widely
practiced Old Order Amish customs. As one person remarked during
a conversation with a company of mixed Old and New Order couples,
"They're *very* Amish." Another knowledgeable observer of the differences between Amish settlements has even postulated that the gap between the Old Order Amish and the Swartzentrubers may be as great as
the gap between most evangelical Christians and the Old Order Amish.

Some of this my husband already knew, but he wanted to find out
for himself what sort of people they are. So he set about trying to meet
them. However, this proved to be more difficult than he had anticipated,

and his affability and persistence went unrewarded. When he stopped to purchase eggs at a Swartzentruber farm, typically he would be greeted by a farmwife from a safe position inside her screen door, her children peering from a nearby window. She would respond to him as briefly as possible. On one such trip after stopping at four different farms—and collecting four dozen eggs—he still failed to engage any of the tight-lipped housewives who had sold them to him from their half-opened doors in amiable conversation, one woman with patches on her apron and one wearing a copper ring on her finger as a cure for arthritis.

Then he noticed "Strawberries for sale" scrawled on a sign in a yard of one of the farms and decided to pursue this possibility. In the fading light of the June evening, he edged past the barking dog, entered the dooryard, and approached the side porch. A sixtyish man with a scruffy beard and dusty clothes answered his knock, responding to his questions regarding the availability of strawberries with a slow sideways shake of his head. "They're all gone" was the reply. His unwelcoming demeanor led my husband to believe this was yet another dead end.

But my husband took a deep breath and ventured another question. Identifying himself as a college professor who taught a course on Amish life, he stated that he needed places for his students to live with Amish families for the required homestays. Would he or anyone he knew be willing to take a student or two—for pay, of course?

The man again shook his head. "We wouldn't do that," he murmured.

"I guess it's against your Ordnung," my husband remarked, revealing by his question that he knew more than the typical English person.

"No, but . . . ," and the man paused, fidgeting noticeably. "We just wouldn't do that. Besides, my wife's been sick," he confided. He hesitated, and then for some unexpected reason, disclosed many of the details regarding her illness and the difficult periods the family had experienced as a result. But the man did not invite him inside the house.

My husband listened with genuine sympathy, surprised that the man would share his burdens with a stranger, wondering whether he simply needed a nonjudgmental listener to whom he could reveal his troubles. When the man seemed satisfied that he had explained sufficiently the reasons for his refusal, my husband offered the man a recently published book on the Amish, which he accepted readily.

"Would your bishop know of anyone in the district who would be willing to keep a student or two?" My husband inquired, knowing that the bishops often set the standard for what is accepted behavior in the district.

By then it was too dark for my husband to discern the expression on the man's face, but the vocal response was a soft laugh.

"I *am* the bishop," came his reply.

"*You* are the bishop?" my husband repeated, staring at that man who didn't seem very bishoplike in appearance.

Soon he was relating his story. As a young man he had decided to leave the Amish—after joining church, which is always serious. This means that the delinquent church member will be placed under the ban and shunned by members of his family and community. Shunning by the Swartzentruber group would be especially severe, my husband knew. So he ran away from home and joined the armed forces, not coming back to visit because of the tensions this created between him and his parents and the church. However, during that time his mother continued to set his place at the dinner table, ever hopeful that he would return. As he spoke, he shifted position uncomfortably but still looked my husband in the eye.

"I was in the Air Force for four years," he stated flatly.

My husband couldn't believe either his eyes or his ears. This prototypical Swartzentruber Amish elder with the prototypical beard and bearing had just confessed that he had spent four years in a military force representing the complete antithesis of everything Amish persons of all varieties stand for. No Amish person denies his nonresistant stance regarding war and remains Amish. By definition all Amish are nonresistant.

"You had guns?" my husband inquired with astonishment.

A slow nod, and then, "Yes."

"Where did you spend most of your time?" asked my husband, trying to visualize this Amishman in precise military attire somewhere around the globe.

"In Japan."

My husband paused to absorb this information. Then his questions came quickly. "How did this happen? What made you leave? Why did you join a branch of the military?"

His host thought for a moment, pondering the events of many years ago. Then he replied slowly, "I always liked to read—maybe that's what got me into trouble."

He thumbed the pages of the book my husband had given him as he replied, as though eager to read what new judgments the outside world was making about the customs of his people.

"How did you get back?" my husband asked.

"Oh, I knew I would have the benefits of the GI bill, so I decided to apply to college when my term of duty was over. I was accepted in the school of engineering in a university."

"What happened next? Did you go?" my husband queried.

"I decided to visit my parents one more time before going off to college. I wanted to let them know what was happening in my life. But when I came down the lane, I realized that here was where I belonged. So I came back." His voice was bland and matter-of-fact. "And here I am," he smiled faintly.

"What's the rest of your life been like?" inquired my husband.

He shrugged. "Pretty much like other Amish. I became a minister in a couple of years. I married and had nine children, two still at home. Then a few years back I was chosen bishop."

Anticipating my husband's next question he shook his head slowly sideways and looked him squarely in the eye.

"No regrets," he declared firmly.

He suggested a non-Swartzentruber family that might take in some of my husband's students—and they did. He also consented to speak with my husband's class, showing just how unruffled he is by the world outside the Amish enclave, a world he has experienced and rejected and finds neither threatening nor alluring.

For more than an hour he described Swartzentruber customs and answered the students' questions in a soft and unhurried manner. Finally, when he appeared to be finished, my husband asked him whether there was anything special he would like to say to the group before they left.

He pondered for a moment, then looked at the students whose dress suggested that they were living in a century far removed from the one he occupied.

"Well," he replied quietly, "I think I'd like to say that I don't think it's necessary to be Amish to get to heaven. But if you are Amish"—and here his voice became louder and firmer—"I think you should stay Amish and be the very best Amish person you can."

ᵛ∿ 14 ∿

Plain People's Paradise?

An Amish "snowbird" community? An Amish winter resort? A place catering to pleasure and leisure, the antithesis of the Amish values of work and frugality? Sounds preposterous, I think. But my husband, who has already visited fifty Amish settlements in more than a dozen states, wants to experience this one. He has heard rumors that have piqued his curiosity, and he wants to check them out. So one day in late December we find ourselves tooling along the sunlit, citrus and palm tree-edged streets adjacent to the intersection of the main thoroughfares of Beneva and Bahia Vista in the section of Sarasota, Florida, known as Pinecraft. We deposit our belongings at the two-room apartment where we will be staying and head for the nearby park, which we have been told is the center of activities during this interlude between the holidays.

As we pass through streets named for the early settlers who came to work in the celery farm and vegetable patches established here over seventy years ago, we decide they might better be labeled, "Caution: People Everywhere," and that the speed limit ought to be ten miles an hour at most. A small barefooted boy clad in black pants with the traditional suspenders rides a two-wheeler. Beyond him two plain-clothed teen-aged boys speed smoothly along on Rollerblades. They almost run into a group of white-capped, giggling young women attired in plain dresses of green and purple and shades of blue, who scatter quickly as they race by. An elderly couple glide along leisurely on three-wheeled bicycles, each with sacks of groceries in the wire baskets behind their seats. They wave and call to another couple sitting on lawn chairs in front of their neat but diminutive cottage. I remember that bicycles are not permitted according to the Ordnung in Lancaster County, Pennsylvania, although Rollerblades are. In contrast, most Ohio and Indiana Amish groups frequently employ bicycles as a means of transportation.

"Where are the horses and buggies?" I inquire.

My husband raises his eyebrows in the way he reserves for times when I have said something especially stupid.

"Did you really think the city of Sarasota would permit horses and buggies inside its limits?" he asks. "What would they do with all that horse dung—all the mess and smell and health hazards?"

I don't answer. I'm too busy watching two little old ladies in their white prayer coverings and long black skirts maneuver their three-wheelers past a van crowded with plain Mennonites and toward an open grassy area ahead. I hear sporadic bursts of shouting and applause, as though some game might be in progress.

It is, in fact. In the small park edged by mobile homes and one-story houses, on a sand volleyball court, Amish, plain Mennonites, and English compete vigorously while spectators in both plain and English clothes cheer them on. Cars, vans, trikes, and bikes jam the streets around the park's perimeter, and we work our way through the crowd of onlookers to get a better view. Smack! smack! goes the ball, back and forth. I wonder how the girls, barefoot and wearing long dresses, can so deftly lob it over the net, but they do. Although most of the fellows are wearing plain clothes, at least they aren't as encumbered as the females are. We soon ascertain that the skills displayed here demonstrate that they do more than forking manure, chopping wood, and heisting lumber to build athletic prowess.

Upon inquiry, we are told that contests involving various groups are scheduled in a quasi tournament during this period when families with children have escaped from both the weather and the responsibilities of their homes up north. Although Pinecraft developed into a combination retirement community/health resort in the midcentury, in recent years it has also attracted a fair number of young people, not just those who are vacationing with their families, but also some who have left their home settlements to explore the world beyond. However, they do not always have the blessings of their parents or the bishops of their home districts in this venture. Watching the youth at play and the assortment of individuals cheering them on, we wonder what stories they have to tell.

Of course, my husband is already talking with the Amishman standing beside him, and soon he discovers that they have mutual friends. The two of them smile and laugh and shake hands. Then my husband asks whether a retired Amish couple from a Midwest community happens to be in Pinecraft; he's heard they like to winter here, maybe even spend as much as six months away from the snow and cold. Yes, the man replies, giving the name of the street where they reside. They love to have visitors.

People, after all, are mostly what Pinecraft is about. If you're Amish and you've come here because you have the freedom to get away from it all, you have plenty of time to participate in the favorite pastime of Amish adults, especially the older ones. Which is, of course, to visit. Here without televisions, radios, tape or CD players, the Internet, or prescribed tasks and schedules, there is plenty of time. Since church members are not allowed to play cards or lounge on the beach—and certainly not to sunbathe—you spend much of your time talking with friends, new and old. Pinecraft is a cozy, comfortable retreat where you can talk face to face with people you've read about in the Amish periodicals, *The Diary, The Budget,* or *Die Botschaft*—or with people you've visited infrequently because of the intervening distances back home. Here they are just down the street or around the corner.

You visit while walking to the post office, while bent over a quilt stretched out in a garage, or while competing at shuffleboard in the park. Stopping by an Amish friend's house one morning, my husband is informed that he has gone off to "shuffle," and when my husband later tries the sport himself, he is soundly beaten by a meek-mannered but very practiced Amish grandmother.

Naturally, you visit in each other's "homes," those temporary residences that are owned or rented, but which become "yours" for a few days or weeks or months during the winter season. When someone stops by your small cottage or mobile home, you drop whatever you are doing and chat, sometimes offering popcorn or coffee or cookies along with the news of the day—people news, mostly—the weather back there, the good fortunes or misfortunes of mutual friends, and your acquaintances who will be coming down on the next bus. Of course you also play the "who-do-you-know-that-I-know" game.

One elderly couple reports that they had one thousand visitors sign their guest book last winter, but were down to eight hundred this season. While only approximately a dozen Amish families reside year round, the population in Pinecraft proper, which is less than a mile square, swells to at least two thousand during the peak period in late December, January, and February. One winter resident estimates that when the Mennonites on the other side of Beneva are included in the tally, it rises to over four thousand.

Although many of the inhabitants of Pinecraft are Amish, vacationers from other Anabaptist persuasions also congregate here, including those from the more liberal New Order, Beachy Amish, and conservative Mennonite groups. For this reason, some Amish bishops forbid their people to come here, and to the more conservative Amish, anyone who indulges in more than a cursory visit is suspect.

Outside of church these groups meet and mingle, not only in each other's living rooms, on the streets, and the park, but also in the restaurants that cater to Pennsylvania Dutch palates. The boundaries are ignored particularly at *Troyers' Dutch Heritage Restaurant*. Arising early for breakfast, my husband joins English and Amish locals in the back room of the restaurant for coffee and conversation. When my husband asks an acquaintance with whom he is sharing a table how many persons present probably could speak Pennsylvania Dutch, he replies, "Oh, I'd say about 99.9 percent—regardless of the kind of clothes they're wearing." English neighbors living next to the Amish in Pinecraft almost always have Amish relatives or have themselves defected from the Amish church.

Neither of us speaks Pennsylvania Dutch, but that does not stop us from exploring the neighborhood and making friends, since everyone here also speaks English. We bike along streets named Graber, Kauffman, and Yoder, good Amish names that fit with those on the mailboxes—Beiler, Gingerich, Fisher. But we wonder how other streets became Clarinda, Gardenia, and Hacienda instead of Bontrager, Stoltzfus, and King. We stroll past front yards containing boxes or bags of grapefruits and several varieties of oranges with hand-lettered "For Sale" signs listing the prices beside them. Often a shoebox or Tupperware container rests beside them, partially filled with bills and coins so that customers can make their own change. Pinecraft feels like a safe place where doors and windows may be left open, at least during the day. Someone is always next door or across the way if help is needed. But the settlement is not impervious to the intrusion of outsiders, and occasional tales of stolen bicycles and fishing equipment suggest that maybe the doors should be locked after all.

In such a high-density setting, it can take a long time to get from here to there, but that's part of the fun. One bright afternoon during a bike ride, we notice a crowd gathered in the parking lot of the "Tourist Church," a centrally located conservative Mennonite place of worship. Then we remember that this is the day when the bus containing Amish vacationers is scheduled to arrive from up north, one of several that bring Amish persons from Ohio, Indiana, and Pennsylvania. During the peak season, hired vans also regularly carry passengers from Illinois and other distant points, and some New Order Amish even fly down.

Curious, we pedal faster, passing a Beachy Amishman who calls, "Looks like an auction, doesn't it?" Laughing, we agree. A few paces further we meet an Old Order Amishman who declares, "Looks like a fair," and then excuses himself while he moves off in search of a friend he thinks will be on the bus.

Indeed, the gathering does have a holiday atmosphere. The area behind the church and the streets adjoining it are a welter of bikers, trikers, and walkers. Pennsylvania Dutch and English alike fly along with a lot of laughing and gesturing. The scene will be repeated when the bus leaves the next day or so carrying Amish snowbirds back up north. Typically people begin assembling an hour or so before the bus arrives or departs, suggesting that the Amish feel no one should come or go on long trips without the support of friends and family.

During our stay we visit in a number of the homes, where we discover that the most obvious difference between the Amish lifestyle up north and here in the sunny south is in the level of technology permitted. Unlike Old Order Amish settlements elsewhere, the use of electricity is almost universal in Pinecraft, whether the residents come from an Old Order district, which forbids it, or whether they identify with the New Order Amish, among which Ordnungs vary. This means that refrigerators, freezers, and even microwaves are standard equipment, and in at least some houses, cable television hookups are available, perhaps because the houses are sometimes rented to English persons during the off-season in addition to the tourist season. Only once during our walks around the community did we observe a propane lamp in use.

Likewise, telephones are ubiquitous, not discreetly hidden in some building at the end of a lane, but openly displayed on the wall or table and just as openly used. We are astonished to find that one of our Amish friends not only has several phones, but that one of them is a speakerphone equipped with caller ID. We spot a number of Amish persons talking on cell phones. One Amishwoman complains that when she talks to her neighbors back home in Shipshewana, Indiana, they relay her "news" via phone to the neighbors down the street in Pinecraft before she can. And a directory that lists the names of Amish members of settlements in the southern states also gives the phone numbers of Pinecraft residents. This is different from most settlements "back home," where having telephones in the house is against the Ordnung.

Old Order Amish winter residents still look and act Amish, however, at least most of the time. I enjoy trying to identify the geographical area the various women come from by the differences in their head coverings and clothing. I also wonder what they think as they work and play with Anabaptist groups whose dress standards are more lenient or more strict, among them modern Mennonites wearing short hair, short skirts, jeans, and jewelry. Driving past a bus stop near the gulf on Siesta Key, we observe a cluster of young Amishwomen in plain dresses, waiting to return to their Sarasota "ghetto." But we also hear of other youth who abandon traditional clothing and appear in shorts or swimsuits. Of course, news of such behavior drifts to the home districts, and this kind of behavior, as well as the presence of persons with more liberal lifestyles, causes the clucking of many Amish tongues up north. If technology and dress have been compromised, what else is taking place, they wonder. When my husband showed a local Mennonite historian a description he had written about Pinecraft, he passed it on to an Amish winter resident who also read it. "Tell him to scrap it," was his terse response.

Yet another aspect of Amish life that appears to remain the same in Pinecraft is the Sunday morning church service, which is similar to Amish worship services elsewhere. One important difference is that because of the smallness of the Pinecraft houses, the service is always held in the same place, one of the larger houses which has an open, extended first floor permanently equipped with chairs and benches. This building is now designated the "church house." Sometimes members from the north have transferred their membership to it, supposedly because they spend as much time here as in their home districts, but gossips whisper that it is because the standards are less severe. The truth in their accusations was attested to when the entire church became New Order—and subsequently lost a significant number of their members. Presumably the Old Order defectors did not want to be out of favor with their home districts and risk shunning when they returned for the summer. But these changes do not appear to have affected attendance, since six hundred people were present at one service not long after the change, many of them gathering on the lawn outside the church house.

Articles in prominent newspapers have focused on Pinecraft as a winter haven for members of the Amish community, a place of "easy living," a "Plain People's Paradise." And yes, on the surface it is that—a safe and legitimate refuge from the frigid north. But underneath the cozy and comfortable facade lie the inevitable tensions that occasionally bubble up and boil over, suggesting that the currents here run abut the same as they do anywhere that people interact.

Some of the ferment is internal. One scribe reports in *Die Botschaft,* "There seems to be some friction between the Pa. people and the tourists from Ohio and Ind. It so seems the Pa. people have more money and so buy the houses that come up for sale. Then the Pa. tourists have first choice to rent them."[1] One northern Amishman's response to that was, "If it's in the *Botschaft,* it's serious! It's like, whew! Bad music. If that kind of thing continues, Florida is going to become out of bounds. People are doing goofy things down there."

We hear other complaints. Some conservative northern bishops and church members view Pinecraft as a wild place. Past evidence has supported this position, since police have occasionally conducted drug busts and broken up drinking parties in the park. But not infrequently, both of these activities occur in major settlements up north—and these can't be blamed on Pinecraft. Also, if whispers of sexual misconduct travel the grapevine in Pinecraft and beyond, we are not shocked, since we also know that Amish persons up north have been involved in sexual affairs. Perhaps, however, the vacation mentality, the frequent contact with those whose Ordnungs are more liberal, and the distance from restraining influences combine to make Pinecraft especially risky for those who are already "fence-sitters." As one young Amish resident admitted, "It's the fact that we are away from home with no supervision that can lead to trouble."

So, it is not without cause that Pinecraft is perceived by some as "on the edge." For the restless, it can become a temporary stop on their way "up" to "higher" church groups and eventually "out." Depending on the ruling of their home district, many of them can establish membership here without being placed under the ban. Eventually they can safely move on to a conservative Mennonite group, then later to a more liberal Mennonite congregation. As a result, modern Anabaptist churches nearby are home to

1. Letter, *Die Botschaft,* Mar. 17, 1999.

lots of people who have left the Amish faith and now claim to be perfectly contented. Also, Pinecraft appears to attract Amish people whose children are not Amish. One Amishman informed my husband, "I saw Aaron walking with an Englishman, and then I discovered it was his son."

We contemplate what would happen if church authorities declared Pinecraft "off-limits" to members of the major Amish settlements up north. My husband remarks that one Amish friend of ours would have to sell his Pinecraft house. I retort that no, he wouldn't; he's resourceful, he'd find some way out. But realistically, I can't think of how. We know of one Amish couple who was required to sell their Pinecraft residence when the husband was chosen by lot as a minister, and they complied. When I describe to a more liberal Anabaptist friend the possibility of the Old Order communities declaring Pinecraft as "verboten," his immediate reaction is, "Good. Then there will be more room for *us*."

All this is conjecture, I know. But after several visits, I have finally realized that we aren't the disinterested observers of this "Plain People's Paradise" that I thought we were. While we have vacationed here, we have visited with Amish friends within Pinecraft and with Mennonite friends living in the areas adjacent to it. We have attended Bahia Vista Mennonite Church and interacted with its members, joining them for worship and fellowship. We are a part of the mix of northern Anabaptists who have come to Florida seeking solace from the winter's cold. And once again we have observed the inevitable conflicts and complexities that prevent fallible human beings from finding a paradise on earth.

❧ 15 ❧

Old Folks at Home

You must meet them—we've been told many times—this retired couple who, although in their eighties, still write for the Amish newspapers and still welcome a multitude of visitors from across the country in their house up north and in this, their Florida apartment. They have achieved a kind of fame among the Amish communities, and we want to find out why. We also want to learn why older Amish people command so much respect.

A wizened woman with a dowager's hump and a pear-shaped figure answers our knock, her dark eyes sparkling her welcome. Attired in a brown dress closed in front with the traditional straight pins, she is holding a crochet needle and a partially completed afghan. We identify ourselves, and she nods, responding that they had heard we were in the area. Later we learn that not much that happens in the Amish community escapes their attention. She invites us in and introduces us to her husband.

He sits in a recliner in the small sitting area off the kitchen, a slight, wiry elflike figure with a wispy ivory beard, posture and eyes both signaling his alertness and his self-confidence. My husband places a recently published book about Amish life almost under his nose, querying him about where the cover photo was probably taken.

It is a photo of an Amishman harvesting hay with his team, a sight that causes much rubbernecking by tourists who drive through the Amish settlements of Ohio, Pennsylvania, and Indiana, states in which the tourist industry is a kind of parasite feeding on the quaintness of Amish customs and culture.[1]

He assesses it quickly and looks up, remarking sharply, "That's Lancaster County [Pennsylvania]. Those wheels weren't made in our shop. Look at the way the spokes are put together. We don't do it that way," he says with a hint of scorn.

Then he squints again at the photo.

1. Cover photo by Dennis Hughes in Donald B. Kraybill and Marc A. Olson, eds., *The Amish Struggle with Modernity* (Hanover, N.H.: Univ. Press of New England, 1994).

"Sure," he asserts confidently. "Look at those mules and horses—mules on the inside, horses on the outside. Nobody does that where we live."

Mules are commonly used for fieldwork in the extensive and fertile Lancaster County settlement. But some other Amish communities regard the mule as an aberration of nature—an "unnatural" animal since it is a cross between a horse and a donkey. Hence they believe it is wrong to breed and employ mules in their work.

I glance down at the old-fashioned cardboard fan with its popsicle stick handle that our host has given me and turn it over to the back on which the advertisement for his carriage shop business has been printed. It lists his name, address, and his claims as "Mfg. of Farm Equipment," "Machinists," and "Steel Fabricators."

I wonder what kind of power they use for their equipment and whether a blacksmithing area is included along with the carriage manufacture. I know that he is pleased to tell his visitors that a man from a foreign country spent several months living and working with him and his family, learning the rudiments of carriage construction and repair so that he can use the knowledge and skills he has acquired in the construction and maintenance of carriages back home.

The patriarch feels good about his life's work, about what he knows and has accomplished, about his services to his own settlement and the respect that he has won from the broader community beyond it. He does not say so, but the erectness of his posture and the confidence of his voice make me sense it.

He coughs several times, attempts to phrase a sentence, and then rises and goes over to the sink, draws a glass of water, and adds one or two drops of peppermint flavoring to it. He is, I will find out later, very health conscious.

"Gotta have something to stop this coughing," he explains as he lifts the glass and swallows.

"Maybe you should take some cough syrup," his wife Annie suggests. She leans forward in her rocking chair and interrupts her rhythmic crocheting, needle poised in air. "You've had that cough for a month now."

We wait for him to recover his voice. I look back down at the advertisement on the fan and note that in addition to his listing of skills and services he has added "Historian."

It seems a bit out of place among the descriptions relating to steel fabricating, machinery, and horse-drawn vehicles. But then, I do not think like an Amish person. A historian, in my context, is one who spends long years cooped up in a library pouring over dusty tomes, ferreting out evidences for theories regarding the social and political movements of the larger society. A historian travels to places where cataclysmic events such as battles have taken place, collecting evidence to verify those theories—weighing, cataloging, proposing, revising.

How does an Amish historian function, I wonder. I have only to listen to him talk with my husband to find out. They are discussing the origins of the settlement of which our host is a member. He knows who moved there first and when, which farm he bought, who his father was, who he married and who his sons and daughters married, how many children they had, and when one church district divided from another and why.

Like other Amishmen we know, he enjoys tracing family relationships. Sometimes this kind of "history" can become very convoluted. For example, one *Botschaft* letter announced a local death like this: "John died suddenly January 28. John served as preacher for forty-two years. John's wife was in Doddy Dan's relation. Her mother Sarah Stoltzfus married to Jake Stoltzfus was grandmother Emma's niece. A daughter of David Beiler's Mary, the second wife of Amos Esh. This is the Mary that was the second wife of Benuel King. It's a bit difficult to describe that family and how they are related." (Only the names, dates, and some minor grammatical errors have been changed in this account.)

Our host is a repository of the history of his home community. He illustrates an important aspect of Amish society: Whereas in the larger Western civilization, wisdom resides in books, in the Amish community, "wisdom" is usually transmitted orally. However, when questioned, Jake admits that he has recently written a brief history of an Amish settlement in another state. He wonders why they didn't write it for themselves.

Still, he is guarded in what he divulges, cautious about us, his new English acquaintances. He plies us with questions, wanting to find out what we already know about Amish life. He expresses surprise when he realizes we are aware of specific Amish customs, for example, bed courtship, or bundling, as it is frequently called. He is, we sense, determined to put the Amish community in the best light since he is not certain how we might use the information he reveals. We understand.

The conversation turns to the Amish newspapers, *The Budget*, published in Sugarcreek, Ohio, and *The Diary* and *Die Botschaft*, which originate in Lancaster County, Pennsylvania. Jake writes for two of the papers and his wife, Annie, for the other, each reporting the family and church events in their community—everything from the weather and the state of the crops to births, deaths, accidents, and visits by friends and relatives from other settlements. Annie gives us copies of one of the papers, telling us that she has cut out her articles—which, of course, are the very ones we want to read most.

Businessman that he is, Jake complains about the lack of advertising in *Botschaft*.

"I counted twenty-four pages [out of approximately thirty-six] without ads," he declares. "And then they whine because they're running in the red."

But that is not what bothers him most about *Botschaft*.

"It really turns me off when I find misspelled words," he fumes. "The other papers have better editing. If I do misspell a word, the editors of *The Diary* catch it."

Jake has had a poem published on the front page of a recent issue, one that depends primarily on rhythm, rhyme, and pleasant sentiment for its effect. I am relieved that he does not ask our opinion of it and that he does not know that I have taught a college course on poetry. How could I, in a few minutes, possibly explain to him the significance of nuances of connotation, sound, and symbol—the essences out of which the best "literary" poems are created?

And how could he possibly explain to me the delicate balances necessary in manufacturing the carriages that carry him and his fellow Amish constituents on the rounds of their daily lives?

We ask how many children, grandchildren, and great-grandchildren he and his wife have.

"You'll have to speak up louder," Jake instructs us. "Annie is wearing a hearing aid."

"I have to," she explains. "If I didn't, everything would sound like a whisper. I've been wearing a hearing aid for thirty-five years now."

"Ah, now, Annie," Jake grins, "it's been longer than that. You've been saying 'thirty-five years' for at least ten!"

Annie ignores him and begins to compute, murmuring softly. "Nine children, forty-two grandchildren, and—let me see—twenty-two, going on twenty-three great-grandchildren," she reports. "How about you?"

I gasp in astonishment. "We're expecting our first grandchild at the end of this month."

Jake's eyebrows arch with surprise.

"How many brothers and sisters do you have?" he queries.

My husband replies that he has a brother and sister and that I am an only child.

They look at us with pity, obviously feeling sorry for our lack of family. But they refrain from passing judgment, merely murmuring something about our missing out on the joys of having a big family. Silently I calculate their eighty descendants, wondering how long our planet could support such rapid multiplication of human beings. They probably have not considered such an idea, and if they did, they would respond that such things are best left to the Lord, who instructed Adam and Eve to "be fruitful and multiply." Or they might quote the passages from the Psalms which declare that "children are a gift from the Lord" and "happy is the man who has his quiver full of them."

We are interrupted by another set of visitors, an Old Order Mennonite couple, whom Jake and Annie welcome as warmly as they welcomed us. Jake introduces them to us while Annie passes around her homemade chocolate chip cookies and peanut brittle. I wonder if it is appropriate to ask for her recipes.

Sensing that it is time for us to leave, we rise and move toward the door. As we sign their guest book, my husband counts the number of visitors who "dropped by" on New Year's Day—an impressive total of twenty-six. They invite us to visit them again.

We do. Our friendship flourishes, perhaps because they sense our genuine interest in and admiration for many aspects of Amish society. Knowing Annie is an expert quilter, I show them a quilt I have been working on, hoping that it doesn't look too amateurish. It features various farm figures, among them a barn, a tractor, some cows, and in one square a black Amish horse and carriage.

Jake identifies the pink pig in one square as a Duroc and then turns his attention to the horse and buggy.

"That's a Lancaster County buggy," he mutters. "Look at the back part. We don't make them that way in Indiana."

"Who's going to quilt it for you?" Annie asks.

I hesitate. I know she quilts like a machine—I've seen her work. I'm the understudy here: the learner. My degrees mean nothing in this setting. What I'm ashamed to admit is that I've never quite mastered holding a needle and thimble and moving my fingers and thumb back and forth in the proper manner to achieve a smooth, even, and closely spaced series of stitches across the layers of fabric and batting. I still resort to the regular running stitch.

"I could quilt it for you," she suggests. "But it would have to be when I get back home. You could send it UPS."

Jake looks again at my quilt. "It would be a piece of cake for her," he says proudly.

It will take me forever, I know, although I'd like to try. Maybe I should pay Annie to quilt it. But I hesitate to have her see how badly sewn together it is—how many mistakes I've made. I feel like a kindergartner in the school of quilt making.

Observing Jake and Annie across several weeks, I am impressed with their sense of significance, a term that they probably would not consider using in connection with themselves, believing such ideas to be indicative of *Hochmut* (pride). The way Amish communities integrate their older members into their daily lives reminds me of some principles which the speaker in a session on Anabaptist life and thought emphasized as basic to Anabaptist community. These are that all people are of extreme value, the welfare of the whole exceeds the welfare of the individual, everybody has something to contribute to the whole, and differences in giftedness are not equivalent to differences in worth. While few Amish persons would articulate these ideals if asked, they are lived out in such a way—albeit imperfectly—that they are absorbed along with home-baked bread and shoofly pie.

In the Amish communities older people are not relegated as worn-out discards to some nursing home scrap yard. Sometimes they are taken into the family of one of their children; sometimes a separate addition or even a smaller house is built on the homestead for them. So common is this practice that the building is commonly referred to as a *Grossdawdy Haus* (granddaddy house).

The naturalness of the interaction between generations is highlighted for me one evening when we stop to visit Jake and Annie and find once again that they already have company. Annie is playing a board game with their married grandchildren and some friends, all in their late teens and early twenties. Their great-grandchildren, aged one and three, are playing with toys under the table and climbing on Jake's lap.

A day or two later when I greet Annie riding her adult tricycle on the street, she reports that their grandchildren left on the bus for home that afternoon. For only a moment I detect a slight lessening of her usual sparkle. We chat a few minutes about her latest quilting project. Then, knowing we will be leaving before daylight the next day, she wishes me a safe trip back north and urges me to visit them again next year.

I wave as Annie deftly maneuvers her trike into her yard. Sometime, I decide, I might even get bold enough to ask for her recipe for peanut brittle.

~ 16 ~

In Unison or Harmony?

We are sitting in an Old Order Amish meetinghouse, listening to an Amish historian describe worship in this Pennsylvania county as it has been practiced for more than two hundred years. Amish meetinghouses are rare, and this particular settlement is remarkable for having them. In most Amish communities, Sunday services are held every other week in the house, barn, or workshop of a family in the district. The members here do not call the building where they worship the "church"; rather it is the "church" that meets here, hence the term "meetinghouse." Our speaker details the customs of this particular settlement beginning with which door the women and children enter and which the men and boys use, why the ministers do not sit up front facing the assemblage but on the same level as the laypeople, and where the congregants sit according to age and sex.

My fellow listeners include about fifty Amish men and women who have come by bus from a distant county, intently absorbing the similarities and differences between this settlement and their own. The similarities are much more marked than the differences; Old Order Amish worship customs have probably changed less than any other aspect of Amish life.

Suddenly in the relaxed interchange of questions and answers, one of the men, knowing that the speaker is a song leader in the local district, requests that he sing a few lines of "Lob Lied" (praise song), the song that is the second one sung during every Sunday morning service in each Amish worship service. Modestly he objects; then at the urging of several others he begins the slow, somber lines in German. The men and women in front of him sit in silence, intent upon words and music, pace and interpretation.

Sometimes the singing of four or five stanzas of a single hymn from the *Ausbund,* the Amish hymnal dating back to 1564, can take twenty to twenty-five minutes. When one of my Amish friends questioned me about my reaction to the singing in a service he knew I had attended, I avoided answering. Accustomed to four-part harmony, I was at first intrigued and later turned off by this unison style of singing with its wandering up and down among several notes for each syllable of a word. To my uninitiated English ears it seemed a cross between a Gregorian chant and a bagpipe dirge. How, I wondered in my ethnocentric ignorance as I attempted to follow the unfamiliar German text, could a culture that has produced such musical giants as Bach, Beethoven, and Brahms produce a music as mournful as this? Only after repeated exposure have I come to recognize its peculiar kind of beauty.

Our leader is not performing; he is savoring both tones and words. Even though this is an informal Saturday gathering rather than a structured Sunday worship service, I sense that he is intent upon meaning—and for the first time I realize how much the form is an integral part of that meaning. What seemed to me to be a fault in the singing is instead part of its very essence. No wonder one of the issues that caused a large split in this settlement about one hundred years ago involved an argument over the singing of four-part harmony. Significantly, the four-parters left; the singers of the traditional Amish style still worship here, singing in unison the hymns of their ancestors.

This unison singing of the melody, somber and measured, is a metaphor for the Amish way of life with its goal of serving God wholeheartedly in community, based on the community's—not the individual's—understanding of the scriptures. Anything that detracts from the practicing of this goal must be expunged from Amish life. Despite its flaws and failures, the Amish vision at its best endeavors to take literally the commands of scripture as it understands them. Committed Amish persons attempt to live out the two-edged thrust of James 1:17, a verse they know well: "Religion that God our Father accepts as pure and faultless is this: to look after the orphans and widows in their affliction and to keep oneself from being polluted by the world" (NIV).

The community's interpretation of scripture as expressed in the local Ordnung is paramount over that of the individual. Even if Amish persons would prefer to have a telephone in the house, to own an automobile, or to employ more modern farm machinery, once they have joined church, most will not do so. Their ideal is to live, as they sing, in unison, even when they personally disagree with a particular rule. Such commitment, of course, is often not arrived at easily. Hence the decision to "join church" may be delayed for some Amish young persons while they pursue the forbidden pleasures of mainstream American culture during the Rumspringa period. Of course there are always those who will find ways of circumventing the Ordnung.

The other criticism Englishers frequently level at the Amish community concerns the restraints placed on freedom and creativity. This is best answered by understanding the Amish perspective. A different kind of freedom exists in a society in which the goal is to blend in rather than stand out, to contribute to the family and community rather than to differentiate oneself from it. This means that the Amish need not expend time and energy attempting to be the top—the number one soccer player, the homecoming queen, the valedictorian, the outstanding farmer of the year. Ideally they do not waste physical and emotional energy climbing a socially imposed status ladder. Instead, each person works to become a contributing member of a community, a goal that is attainable within clearly defined boundaries. If one can accept those boundaries, he or she can develop the confidence that comes from achieving competence in the specific tasks associated with the traditional roles assigned by the community.

Since every vocation has value, every person engaged in meaningful work has value, and those who cannot work because of some disability are still valued because they are creations of God. In Amish society, such persons are considered "special" people, in the best sense of the word. In addition, because Amish society stresses tradition rather than novelty, people and customs become more valued as they age. This is the antithesis of mainstream American society, with its planned obsolescence, emphasis on youth, and insistence on innovation.

The contrast between the attitudes toward clothing in the Amish culture with those in mainstream society illustrates this. Dress in English society is characterized by a strange blend of conformity and individuality. Few people are willing to wear clothes that are very different from those of their peers, yet neither do they want to look exactly like them. I once heard of a homecoming dance at which several girls wore the same kind of dress, which they found mortifying. The girl who related this was relieved that no one was wearing "her" dress. In the Amish community everyone wears clothes cut from the same basic pattern down to the number of pleats, pins, and sleeve length; the significant difference is color—and even that must be within certain limits. Members of mainstream American culture view such restrictions as dull, repressive, and lacking in creativity.

What we often fail to see are the advantages of this "uniform," which include the lack of pressure to prove that one's family has the money to buy expensive clothing, the economy experienced because clothes do not go out of fashion and can be worn out, and the freedom that comes from not having to slavishly follow the latest styles. Modesty, simplicity, and economy become the guiding principles—and, of course, identification with the Amish way of life. They dress, as they sing, in unison.

Those who are less inclined to accept authority and regulation without question are normally the most likely to leave the community. One young woman who left admits that she always read extensively since childhood. She also reports that when at about age five she asked her mother why they dressed as they did, she received the curt reply, "Because we are Amish." She left the community at the age of thirty-one and later completed a college degree, experiencing more of a sense of freedom than of struggle in the process. However, the adjustment can be quite difficult for some ex-Amish. The lack of strong community support and clear lines delineating right and wrong can lead to confusion for the person who has been accustomed to them.

This phenomenon is illustrated in an Amish "novel" *One Way Street*, which depicts the experience of an Old Order Amish youth on his journey away from the faith of his childhood through his association with a conservative Mennonite church and his eventual return to the Amish fold.[1] The complexity of the differences and the disunity he finds among the Mennonites disillusion him. One of the last scenes in the book depicts him back in an Amish worship service, embracing the hymns of his childhood. The book's major thesis is that once the Amish start compromising their way of life, they have started down a one-way street that becomes increasingly liberal and fragmented. I am tempted to dismiss the thesis lightly until I reflect upon a grandmother who still wears the plain garb but whose granddaughter has been caught up with the high school prom scene, the very antithesis of the plain and simple Anabaptist lifestyle.

The fascination with simplicity and the rejection of complexity represented by Amish hymn singing and dress both attracts and repels many of the tourists who visit the major Amish settlements. Even persons more intimately associated with Amish society sometimes experience this attraction-aversion syndrome, often wistfully envying the Amish

1. Elmer Stoll, *One Way Street* (Aylmer, Ontario: Pathway, 1972).

their ability to operate in the world with less complexity and ambiguity, while at the same time becoming exasperated with their inconsistencies and legalism. The producer of a documentary on Amish adolescence described such feelings, and I am aware of these polar reactions within myself as I visit my Amish friends.

After retiring by lamplight to an upstairs bedroom during an overnight visit with an Amish family, I turn on our Walkman radio and listen through the headphones to the full-bodied sounds of a symphony, clear, harmonious, and intricately modulated. Suddenly I want to share this music with the eager-to-learn children I have come to know.

However, radios, symphony concerts, and musical instruments are forbidden, except perhaps for a harmonica in certain communities. I had made a faux pas earlier in the day by admitting that I play the piano and had been greeted with silence. Their instrument of choice is, of course, the human voice singing in chorus—in unison—with other human voices in praise to God. The complexity of a symphony orchestra is beyond their known world. (I wonder how they explain Psalm 150 which portrays worshiping God by using cymbals, trumpets, harps, and dance.)

On another visit we go with parents and children on a bird-watching expedition. As we walk together, Amish and English, down the country road, the father explains to us the Amish practice of arriving at consensus, pointing out that Amish church districts make significant changes in the *Ordnung* only after much discussion and only after reaching unanimity. Until then, he asserts, matters are *unner Sucht,* a Pennsylvania Dutch term meaning "under search," or, he explains, "under study" as in research.

He declares that what is "hidden" must be exposed, particularly if it is unsound, so that it can be corrected and the district can come to agreement. He points out that many splinter groups in other Amish settlements are baffled at how over one hundred Amish districts in his particular county can remain in such close agreement that they remain in communion with each other.

This must be one of those days when my feelings of aversion are stronger than those of attraction, I decide. Of course, I do not express my reactions aloud. But with that kind of mind-set, I grumble to myself, humankind would not have invented the wheel, and primitive sledges would still be pulled by humans because such issues as whether the taming of horses is an appropriate technology would still be "unner Sucht."

In the quiet of our early morning bird walk, I ponder other paradoxes.

Early May is the height of the warbler migration. Warblers are pert creatures so delicately colored and intricately patterned that my husband likens them to pieces of painted china. Dressed in their somber dark outfits all cut from identical patterns, the Amish parents and their children observe the markings of the common yellowthroat with his bandit black mask, exult in the orange breast of the Baltimore oriole glowing from the tip of a tall maple, and peer through a spotting scope at the iridescence of an indigo bunting perched on a telephone wire.

Ever the teacher, my husband points out the sound of the wood thrush singing nearby. "Hear the flutelike call?" he inquires, a comparison that usually enables novices to identify that particular bird. This time, however, his image fails because he has forgotten that the children probably never have heard the clear, fluid notes of a flute, either solo or soaring high above the accompaniment of a full orchestra. Surely unity is expressed in the music of four-part harmony and in the performance of an orchestra, which, although submitting to both conductor and score, still depends upon a diversity of instruments and parts.

I do not know which is easier, to search for that hidden impurity which hinders the goal of singing together the song of life in one voice, or to direct an assemblage of disparate instruments to create a symphony embodying unity in diversity. I only know that on this bright day, as an observer of a creation that is infinitely varied, I look at the Amish and commend but do not embrace their ways of working out the values that we share.

Even now as I write, I hear outside my door the bubbling trill of the house wren, the "meow" of the catbird, and the insistent whistle of the cardinal. From the distance drift the plaintive flutelike tones of the wood thrush. God, I muse, has expressed himself in infinite ways through his creation. To what extent does he also accept our varied responses to him in both worship and lifestyle?

But if I am at times put off by some aspects of Amish life, I am also attracted to other aspects of it, as these ruminations have demonstrated. Again and again I find ways of entering their world. I cherish deeply the many friendships my husband and I have developed with Amish persons. And I am conscious of being made more whole, perhaps even moved toward a simpler, more people-oriented lifestyle because of my contact with Amishness. Nor is this my experience alone; I have heard other Englishers express similar sentiments. Why, I wonder, is this so? Have we missed the harmony that comes with their living in unison, a harmony that those who are so much attuned to the technological and the material often miss?

Amish watching is a favorite tourist activity in the larger Amish settlements. The Amish do not seek us out nearly as often as we seek them out. How do we solve the dilemma of what to retain and what to relinquish from the patterns their lives offer to us? What can we learn from the Amish?

During one of our visits with an Amish family, we found a sheet of paper tacked to the wall of a workshop containing the following admonishment attributed simply to "Uncle Amos":

We realize that not everyone is cut out to be one of the Plain People. Many have not the opportunity. But here is a challenge:

> If you admire our faith—strengthen yours.
> If you admire our sense of commitment—deepen yours.
> If you admire our community spirit—build one.
> If you admire the simple life—cut back.
> If you admire quality merchandise or land stewardship—
> Then make quality.
> If you admire deep character and enduring values—live them.[2]

Later I found out that the "Uncle Amos" who wrote this passage was college educated like at least three other converts I know of—converts who have been attracted enough to the Amish way of life to overcome the obstacles in adapting to it. Something about the Amish lifestyle has been strong enough to cause these college graduates not only to relinquish modern conveniences and to learn the Pennsylvania Dutch language, but also to give up enough of their individual autonomy in order to "sing in unison" with their adopted Amish brothers and sisters: Something beyond the plain and simple. Something most English persons can't comprehend.

2. Robert Alexander, "Uncle Amos," *Small Farmer's Journal* 17 (Summer 1993): 43.

Acknowledgments

With sincere gratitude, I acknowledge the help of many persons in the preparation of this book. They include:

My husband, Richard, who shared with me many experiences and ideas regarding Amish culture, lovingly assured me this book was worth writing and reading, and diverted time from his own manuscript to critique mine.

Our son, Mark, my severest critic in matters of style, who nevertheless insisted that I not give up.

Dorothy Gish, former academic dean at Messiah College, who, upon hearing an early reading of one chapter, challenged me to turn my ideas into a book.

Donald B. Kraybill, former provost at Messiah College, who encouraged and guided me in the writing and publication processes.

Messiah College, which provided the use of its facilities and resources.

Freiman Stoltzfus, who responded to my vision for the book and created illustrations that reflect it.

John L. Ruth, who checked the accuracy of the material in the Amish primer.

The publishing staff at the Kent State University Press, particularly my editor, Joanna Hildebrand Craig, and project editor, Tara C. Lenington.

The many persons who read—and listened to—earlier versions of the book. Their feedback was invaluable in making this book clearer and more accurate.

Our Amish friends and acquaintances, who continue to share their lives with my husband and me, thus refining and enriching our own.